THE COVE

Also by LJ Ross

THE SUMMER SUSPENSE MYSTERIES

1. The Cove
2. The Creek
3. The Bay
4. The Haven

THE DCI RYAN MYSTERIES

1. Holy Island
2. Sycamore Gap
3. Heavenfield
4. Angel
5. High Force
6. Cragside
7. Dark Skies
8. Seven Bridges
9. The Hermitage
10. Longstone
11. The Infirmary (Prequel)
12. The Moor
13. Penshaw
14. Borderlands
15. Ryan's Christmas
16. The Shrine
17. Cuthbert's Way
18. The Rock
19. Bamburgh
20. Lady's Well
21. Death Rocks
22. Poison Garden
23. Belsay
24. Berwick

THE ALEXANDER GREGORY THRILLERS

1. Impostor
2. Hysteria
3. Bedlam
4. Mania
5. Panic
6. Amnesia
7. Obsession

THE COVE

A SUMMER SUSPENSE MYSTERY

LJ ROSS

PENGUIN BOOKS

PENGUIN BOOKS

UK | USA | Canada | Ireland | Australia
India | New Zealand | South Africa
Penguin Books is part of the Penguin Random House group of companies
whose addresses can be found at global.penguinrandomhouse.com

Penguin Random House UK,
One Embassy Gardens, 8 Viaduct Gardens, London SW11 7BW

penguin.co.uk

First published in 2021 by LJ Ross
Published in Penguin Books 2026
003

Copyright © LJ Ross, 2021

Cover artwork by Andrew Davidson

Cover layout by Stuart Bache

The moral right of the author has been asserted

This is a work of fiction. Names, characters, businesses, places, events and incidents are either the products of the author's imagination or used in a fictitious manner. Any resemblance to actual persons, living or dead, or actual events is purely coincidental.

Penguin Random House values and supports copyright. Copyright fuels creativity, encourages diverse voices, promotes freedom of expression and supports a vibrant culture. Thank you for purchasing an authorised edition of this book and for respecting intellectual property laws by not reproducing, scanning or distributing any part of it by any means without permission. You are supporting authors and enabling Penguin Random House to continue to publish books for everyone. No part of this book may be used or reproduced in any manner for the purpose of training artificial intelligence technologies or systems. In accordance with Article 4(3) of the DSM Directive 2019/790, Penguin Random House expressly reserves this work from the text and data mining exception.

Typeset by Riverside Publishing Solutions Limited

Printed and bound in Great Britain by Clays Ltd, Elcograf S.p.A.

The authorised representative in the EEA is Penguin Random House Ireland, Morrison Chambers, 32 Nassau Street, Dublin D02 YH68

A CIP catalogue record for this book is available from the British Library

ISBN: 978–1–804–96039–4

Penguin Random House is committed to a sustainable future
for our business, our readers and our planet. This book is made
from Forest Stewardship Council® certified paper.

PROLOGUE

Natural History Museum, London

"How much longer do we need to keep standing here, grinning like idiots?"

Gabrielle Adams turned to her friend and colleague, whose long, slender body languished against the wall beside her. "Another hour, at least," she said. "There's bound to be more speeches, and there'll definitely be more hands to shake."

The Frenchman Saunders Christmas Party was always a lengthy affair, although the evening had started out well enough, as far as corporate publishing events ever could. As their chosen venue, London's Natural History Museum was resplendent; subtle lighting highlighted its Romanesque arches and intricate tilework, while industrial spotlights shone their bright, mortuary-white glow upon the skeleton of an enormous blue whale suspended overhead, as well as a mastodon and numerous other dinosaur fossils scattered around the central atrium.

The great and the good of the publishing world had gathered to enjoy the bottomless hospitality of one of the United Kingdom's oldest and most revered publishing houses, each jockeying for position to capture the attention of commissioning editors, agents and press hounds who moved amongst them like sharks circling a particularly juicy-looking shoal of unsuspecting fish. Alcohol flowed freely, while canapés flowed rather less so, but few seemed to notice the disparity. A large projector screen had been erected at the top of an impressive stone staircase, upon which an endless slideshow played, showcasing the company's achievements that year and, in particular, the images of those authors currently in favour with the powers that be.

"At least we're allowed to drink red wine, this year," Gabrielle continued. "Last year, the venue told us we weren't allowed to drink anything more pigmented than a gin and tonic, for fear any spillages would damage the marble."

Francesca Ogilvie—better known as "Frenchie", for reasons better left unsaid—let out a muffled groan. "Give me a karaoke bar any day of the week. At least we could let our hair down properly over a few shots and a bad rendition of *Sweet Caroline*. As it is, we've got to spend the next however long listening to a bunch of insecure writers, telling them how bloody great they are," she grumbled. "Oh, God...here comes one of them now."

Gabrielle followed her line of sight and saw a man of around sixty weaving his way through the crowd. Of average height and build, he was unremarkable in every respect, but had made up for it with a liberal choice of attire and—unless she was much mistaken—an even more liberal application of 'Just For Men', which had the desired effect of making its wearer more memorable, albeit for the wrong reasons. She watched him linger on the outskirts of smaller groups of people who had gathered to talk and sip cocktails, whereupon he made several cack-handed attempts to join their conversation. There were some polite nods but, for the most part, he was roundly ignored.

"When was Geoff's last bestseller?" Frenchie wondered aloud. "Six—maybe seven years ago?"

In the mind of the reading public, Geoffrey Bowman was a well-regarded author of spy thrillers whose books had reached many millions of people over the course of his thirty-year career. However, within the rarefied world of publishing, being a household name and recipient of numerous tin-cup trophies for one's writing prowess was not always enough to guarantee the next big advance.

In short, the books still had to sell, and, if they didn't…

It was a slippery slope into the worst kind of hell for a man like Geoff Bowman.

Total obscurity.

Gabrielle watched him make small talk and heard him emit his trademark guffaw, which had once been described by a broadsheet critic as, "a laugh as large as the man's literary talent." Now, sadly, it bore a tinge of desperation and was not shared by the younger members of the group over which he was attempting to hold court.

"It's a fickle business," she murmured. "He's still a good writer, he's just not..."

"Relevant?" Frenchie put in, with a twist of her lips.

Gabrielle sighed. "To a certain audience, he will always be relevant—"

Frenchie snorted. "The man's more of a fossil than that dinosaur bone," she said, gesturing towards one of the displays. "I'm surprised you keep him on your books, when you could have the pick of the bunch."

If Gabrielle detected a touch of envy, she chose to ignore it. "Fundamentally, he can write a good book," she said. "I don't have to like the man to publish his stories—"

"Mayday, *mayday!*" Frenchie interrupted, and knocked back the rest of her drink. "He's spotted us and is making a bee-line. Look, as much as I love you, I don't think I can face listening to Geoff pontificating about the 'Good Old Days' for the next half hour. You're on your own!"

Gabrielle's expression was pained. "Don't you dare—"

Frenchie gave her friend a dazzling white smile, one she knew would absolve her of all sins, and melted into the crowd mere moments before they were set upon.

"Ah, Gabrielle! Just the woman I was looking for."

She turned, her smile already fixed firmly in place, and found herself reciprocating the continental double air-kiss she'd always detested.

"Geoff," she said, once the ministrations were over. "Are you enjoying the party?"

He took a healthy swig of white wine and looked around the room with eyes that were both jaded and hard. "Same every year, isn't it?" he said, clearly unmoved by the impressive architecture of their surroundings. A large Christmas tree stood laden with lights and baubles on the far side of the room, whilst cheesy holiday classics played from hidden speakers, reminding them all to be merry and bright. Tables of drinks manned by white-gloved waiters had been set up, alongside various other gimmicks, such as the 'selfie space' where authors could have their picture taken with the official Frenchman Saunders Publishing backdrop, or the cocktail bar, which served drinks with names taken from the company's most recent list of bestselling titles.

Sadly, none of Geoff's titles had made the cut, so he'd opted for wine instead.

"How's the manuscript coming along?" Gabrielle asked him, and immediately wished she hadn't.

"Oh, slowly...slowly. You know how these things are. You can't rush genius," he said, without any irony whatsoever. "I don't understand this new wave coming up the ranks, you know. They seem to bash out a novel every other week and, lo and behold, the week after, it's a bloody bestseller."

With a cocktail named after it, he added, silently.

"Well, the thing is, Geoff, some writers can be very prolific, which is a good thing for the readers who enjoy their stories," she said, fairly. "It means they don't have to wait so long for the next book to come out."

He snorted. "People should be more discerning," he said, and took another chug of wine.

And you should get off your high horse, Gabrielle was tempted to say, but held her tongue.

"While we're on the subject, I wanted to bend your ear," Geoff said, and moved closer, effectively boxing her in against the wall. "It's about my last advance."

Gabrielle's face became shuttered. "I hardly think this is the time to discuss it," she said, casting a meaningful eye around the room. "Why not give me a call on Monday?"

But Geoff ploughed on. "I'm an international bestseller," he said expansively, getting into his stride. "I've won more awards than almost anybody else in this room, and yet, here I am, slaving away for a pittance. Now, you tell me, is that right? Is it fair?"

She tried to take a sip from her glass, only to find it empty. "Look, Geoff, we've already had this discussion. The advance I offered you, and which you accepted, was based on the most recent performance figures we have to hand. There isn't any easy way to say this but, as you and I both know, the books aren't selling as well as we'd hoped."

He turned a slow shade of puce. "That can only be because the blasted covers are nothing to look at!" he boomed, drawing a few interested glances from those within earshot. "As for the most recent advertising campaign...well, that was a shambles!"

Gabrielle remained silent, choosing not to engage in what had become an age-old debate. When a book didn't sell, there might be many reasons, but the first and most important in her eyes was the quality of the story. As his editor, she'd tried to make the man's most recent efforts the best they could be, but she couldn't work miracles.

"Maybe you should take a break," she suggested. "Have some time to re-group and come back to the manuscript with fresh eyes?"

Bowman favoured her with a fulminating glare, then leaned in to rest an unsteady hand on the wall beside her head.

"Maybe I should just move to another publisher, hmm? What do you say to that?"

Gabrielle stepped deftly out of the way so that he was left to face an empty wall. "You must always do what you feel is best," she said, simply. "Enjoy the rest of the party."

He watched her move off into the crowd, heard the tinkling laughter of women in pink pashminas and men in twill chinos rise up in a cacophony, and felt bile rise to his throat. It was a far cry from the early days, when the air had been filled with cigarette smoke and it had been men like himself who ran the show, not young women barely older than the daughter he hadn't seen for two…no, three years, now. He'd been somebody to reckon with, then. Crowds had parted for him, glasses had been raised for him and every one of the snotty-nosed little chits who now snubbed him would have been clamouring just to spend a sweaty ten minutes in the broom cupboard, on the off-chance he'd put in a good word for them with his agent.

Now…

Now, he had to snivel and beg for what was rightfully *his*.

He'd earned his place amongst these people, damn it. He deserved to have *his* books displayed on the bookcase in the main foyer of Frenchman Saunders, not some little nobody who claimed to be the Next Big Thing.

Perhaps it was time to remind Gabrielle, and her little cohort, of who really pulled the strings.

Gabrielle moved away swiftly, exchanging forced pleasantries as she made her way through the throng towards the ladies' room. It might not be much of a reprieve, but at least there would be a measure of peace and quiet in the relative safety of a toilet cubicle. Her eyes scanned the faces of those she passed, searching for one in particular, but found no sign of him.

She let out a small sigh.

Mark Talbot was a rising star in the world of literary agents, which had been helped in no small part by the fact his grandfather, Marcus Talbot senior, had founded one of the most prestigious literary agencies in London over seventy years ago. That company was Talbot & Co, and, as well as bearing its name, Mark bore a considerable weight of expectation. Many of the authors he represented were at the party that evening, and it was part of his job to pitch new books to her for publication—something which called into question her personal integrity on a regular basis, given that he also happened to be her fiancé.

Unconsciously, her fingers twisted the sparkling diamond ring which adorned the third finger of her left hand.

"Come here often?"

As she stepped into the shadows of the corridor leading to the toilets, a pair of strong arms wrapped around her.

She let out a strangled cry, before realising they belonged to the very person she'd been looking for. "Mark!" she said. "You scared me."

"Sorry, gorgeous," he said, and spun her around to reveal a boyishly handsome face and a pair of over-bright eyes.

"Where've you been?" she asked. "I was looking for you."

"Oh, just doing the rounds," he said, breezily. "Why? Did you miss me?"

He began to edge her back against the wall, nuzzling her neck.

"Mark...stop it. *Mark*, somebody might see!"

"So what? That's what Christmas parties are all about..."

She gave a nervous laugh and pressed a firm palm against his chest. "Mark, this is my work—I have to be professional."

He ran a frustrated hand through his hair, which tended to flop over his forehead, before holding both hands up in surrender. "I forgot," he said, with an edge to his voice. "Work comes first, these days, doesn't it?"

Gabrielle frowned. "That's not fair, I—"

"You don't have to go into it," he said, brusquely. "If you want to stick to shop talk, I need to speak to you about Saffron, as a matter of fact."

Saffron Wallows was Mark's most prestigious client. She wrote 'high concept literature' featuring tortured, downtrodden female characters who tended to meet an unsavoury end, more often than not. Though the general line in their business was that writing about violence against females was not *de rigueur*, hers invariably managed to slip through the net on account of the higher, more important messages she intended to convey.

Or so said the party line.

"I'd have thought you'd be a lot more excited about the opportunity I'm giving you," Mark said, when she didn't respond. "I could go to any of the Big Five and they'd bite my hand off to publish her next masterpiece."

He referred to the coven of publishing giants, every one of them a competitor.

"You know the reason I'm not interested," she reminded him.

He stepped away and stuck his hands in his pockets, surveying her with barely concealed impatience. "Not that rubbish again?"

She folded her arms across her chest, thinking of their most recent argument. "I've already told you, Mark. I'll pass."

"Have you spoken to your boss about it? How d'you think Jacinta will feel when she hears about your decision? Frenchman Saunders has published Saffron's work since the nineties."

Gabrielle had indeed thought about it. Trying to come up with of a way out of their predicament had cost her many a sleepless night.

"Please, Mark. I'm trying to help you…to help us both. Don't force my hand."

He stared at her for long seconds, his face no longer the playful mask it had once been. "Is that a threat?" he said, very softly.

Gabi ran a tired hand over her eyes, then shook her head.

"Of course, it isn't. But I think you should reconsider what I told you the other night, that's all. It's bound to come out, sooner or later, and I'd rather not have to be the one to blow the whistle."

They faced one another in the shadows of the empty corridor, while George Michael sang balefully about giving someone his heart last Christmas.

"How much longer are you going to stay?" Mark asked.

"At the party?"

He nodded.

"I was planning to get the last tube home from South Ken," she replied, and automatically checked her watch.

Eleven thirty-five.

The last train from South Kensington station was at around quarter to one, she knew, and was only a five-minute walk from the museum. That left plenty of time to make the obligatory farewells and administer as many air kisses as required.

"I'll see you at home, then," Mark said, and left without a backward glance.

Gabrielle saw nothing of Mark after that and, since there was no sign of Frenchie either, she decided to call it a night. The alcohol had lost its taste, and what had once seemed festive and glossy now appeared garish and overdone. The crowd was starting to dwindle, and although it might have been expected of her to remain until all her company's guests had departed, fatigue had overtaken any finer sensibilities and she was eager to get home.

But not before the obligatory farewells.

In the end, it took another forty minutes to work her way around the room, thanking this person and that, promising to call others on Monday to arrange lunch, and, by the end of it all, her head was throbbing and her feet aching in the heels she'd worn for style rather than comfort. When she stepped out of the main entrance to the museum and into the brisk December air, it felt like a balm to her overheated skin, and she stood for a minute or two breathing it in. Then, gathering her coat around her, she made her way along Exhibition Road towards the station, her mind lost in thought.

What kind of mood would Mark be in when she got home?

The flat they shared was in the Fulham area, which was only a couple of stops away from South Kensington, on the District line. As a Londoner, born and bred, Gabrielle harboured none of the fears that might have plagued the tourists who passed through London's city streets, although she kept an alarm on her at all times and remained vigilant when walking alone. She still used public transport because, in all her twenty-eight years, she hadn't experienced anything worse than having a mobile phone stolen.

All the same, when she caught sight of the headline plastered across the front page of one of the free daily newspapers left in a stack outside the station entrance, it gave her pause:

TUBE KILLER STRIKES AGAIN

Gabrielle hesitated, thinking of the recent reports of two women having been pushed onto the train tracks by an unknown assailant who remained at large.

She checked the time.

Twelve-forty.

In another five minutes, the last train would have come and gone.

She looked around her, at the street with its closed shop windows and barred metal shutters, and felt something she hadn't experienced in a long time.

Fear.

Every shadow might have been a person, every noise might have been the quiet tread of somebody following her home.

She shivered, and quickly brought up an app on her smartphone which allowed her to search for taxis in the vicinity, only to find that the nearest was twelve minutes away. Having already lost a precious two minutes finding that out, she decided to stop jumping at shadows and fumbled around her bag for her tube pass. Her fingers brushed against the jingling metal of her key chain and, grasping them in one hand and the pass in the other, she made her way hurriedly through the turnstiles and into the station.

Her feet clattered against the metal treads of the long escalator leading down to the platform level, its mechanism whining and clanking as it moved in a continuous loop. She saw nothing but her own reflection, little more than a flash of moving colour against the dull silver-panelled walls, heard nothing but her own blood thundering in her ears while her legs pumped as fast as they could.

Mind the gap...

Gabrielle heard the loud, automated message signalling that the doors of a train were about to close and left the escalator at a run, prepared to make a final dash.

Only to find that the train sitting there like a quiet sentinel was ready to depart from the opposite platform.

She slowed to a walk, her breath condensing on the air in small clouds while her heart rate returned to normal, her fingers relaxing on the keys she still clutched in her hand. Peering through the windows of the train, she found it surprisingly empty, its occupants consisting mostly of security guards returning home from long shifts, or single travellers slumped against Perspex dividers, their eyes already drooping shut. Given the time of year, she'd expected to find the platform teeming with people but, instead, there was only herself and one or two others scattered at intervals.

Tube killer strikes again…

An image of the headline flashed into her mind, and she wondered again whether it had been wise to travel alone.

Mark hadn't offered to take her home.

Sudden tears filled her eyes, followed by immediate anger at her own weakness. She didn't need a man to take her home, did she? Perhaps, had they not been rowing so much lately, he might have come back with her as he always used to, but she was a grown woman and could take care of herself.

She repeated the words inside her head, like a mantra.

The truth was, she'd blown everything out of proportion, and there was nothing to be frightened of—not really. Sure, it made for a sensational headline, but there were eleven tube lines in London, stretching over something in the region of two hundred and fifty miles, according to the game of Trivial Pursuit she'd been forced to play as a kind of team-building exercise in the conference room back at Frenchman Saunders' head office. That was a lot of ground for one lone madman to cover, and the chance of their being in the same place at the same time was very low indeed.

Buoyed by her own logic, Gabrielle took a few deep breaths and watched the train move away from the opposite platform, her eyes locking with those of a woman of around her own age, before the carriage picked up speed and disappeared into the night.

The concourse was quiet in the wake of its departure, and she watched the electronic board for any update on the whereabouts of her own train, which was now running late.

The train to Wimbledon is delayed by three minutes...

Three minutes. That was nothing, in the scheme of things, was it?

And yet...

Yet the night air whipped around her, crawling through the layers of her clothing to trail across her skin like icy tentacles. The platform was eerily silent, lone figures standing too far away for her to make out distinguishing features, such that they all melted into the same face in her mind: the face of an unknown man who was prepared to kill.

Shivering badly now, she scuttled back against the wall, keeping beneath the bold yellow strip-lights and near to the escalators, far back from the platform edge.

Two minutes...

Her eyes darted left…right…then over her shoulder.

Nobody.

She found herself thinking of what Geoff Bowman might have made of her situation, and a bubble of laughter escaped her lips. She could see herself through his eyes—pale and frightened, huddled against the backdrop of an old poster advertising homeopathic remedies for stress—and made a mental note to suggest it to him as a potential plotline, perhaps for a farce.

One minute…

She rubbed her arms and swayed from one foot to the other, counting down the seconds in her head. Suddenly, there came a rush of cold air and the distant rumble of an oncoming train, again from the opposite platform at her back. Turning, she watched the last northbound train shriek into the station and, to her relief, this time it was full of passengers. A moment later, they spilled out of its doors, groups of chattering men and women filling the empty space with sound and colour, and their presence made a mockery of her previous fears.

With the comforting stream of people at her back, Gabrielle turned away to stare into the gaping darkness of the tunnel on her own platform, knowing that, any moment now, the train would arrive. Her eyes traced the tattered posters on the walls touting everything from upcoming concerts to Saffron Wallows' latest book, for which she'd been awarded the Women's Prize for Fiction.

Did she have to see that woman's name everywhere?

Yes, Gabrielle thought, dully. And she had only herself to blame for that.

Lost in thought, the roar of carriages echoing through the blackened tunnel startled her and she watched as twin yellow headlights appeared through the gloom like cats' eyes, sending rats and mice scurrying for cover from the great metal beast.

With only seconds to go, she moved closer to the platform edge, feet shuffling forward on autopilot while the rush of cold, dirty air that preceded the train whipped her hair around her head.

A second was all it took for her life to change.

Even as her hand lifted to brush the hair from her eyes, Gabrielle felt the air leave her body. Her heart gave a single lurch, slamming against the wall of her chest as one strong hand planted itself in the small of her back and pushed—hard.

Suddenly, she was falling…falling…weightless for an endless moment before the ground rushed up to meet her, a deafening scream of brakes drowning out the sickening crunch of bone and flesh as her body crumpled onto the tracks.

CHAPTER 1

Six months later

Gabrielle awoke with a scream.

Arms flailing, legs kicking, she sent a half-empty can of diet coke flying across the aisle of the passenger train, where it fizzed over the sandaled feet of her nearest neighbour. One elbow connected with the window, but she felt no pain; her mind was still far away in another place, at another time.

"*Hey*! Watch it!"

Slowly, the veil lifted, and she became aware of her surroundings, and the chaos she had caused.

"Oh—I'm—I'm so sorry—"

Mortified, face flushed with shame, she fell onto her hands and knees to make a grab for the can, which rolled back and forth beneath the adjoining chairs, its contents seeping into the carpet tile. Feeling the heat of all eyes upon her, Gabrielle snatched it up and beat a hasty retreat towards the relative privacy of the vestibule area, before she could succumb to tears and embarrass herself any further.

She stumbled along the aisle as the train lurched back and forth, her body shaking in the aftermath of yet another daytime terror. The doctors had told her that nightmares would be a perfectly normal response to the trauma she'd suffered but had assured her they'd grow less frequent with time and, naively, she'd believed them. Unfortunately, after six months, vivid memories of the past still invaded her sleep whether during the night or day and intruded into her waking thoughts without any obvious trigger, leaving her perpetually sleep-deprived and anxious, the victim of constantly heightened levels of cortisol and adrenaline.

As Mark had once told her, she was *a paranoid mess.*

Her mind wandered back to that painful exchange, a month or so after she'd returned home from the hospital.

Why couldn't the police get in touch with you, that night? she'd asked him, for the millionth time.

For God's sake, Gabi, give it a rest. I've already told you, my phone battery died, and I went for a walk after the party ended. I needed to clear my head.

But...

But what, Gabi? What are you saying? That I'm having an affair? Is that what you're saying, now?

No, no...

He'd looked at her with something like pity.

I know you've been through something terrible, but you need to get a grip on yourself and move on. Wash your hair, make a bit of an effort, like you used to. You're turning into a paranoid mess.

Even knowing what she now knew—which was, of course, that Mark *had* been having an affair for months—did little to lessen the sting of his words. Like poisoned darts, they'd wormed their way into her heart and made a home there.

Her fingers strayed to her left hand, tracing the thin, pale line where a ring had once been.

I have to beat this, she thought. *I have to beat this, or I'll lose my mind.*

When the doctors had first mentioned the term, 'Post Traumatic Stress Disorder', she'd thought of army veterans who'd been through much greater degrees of trauma than herself. But, as she soon realised, mental health disorders didn't discriminate, and they didn't restrict themselves to certain categories of victim. There was no hierarchy; only an understanding shared by anyone who'd ever had the misfortune to suffer from PTSD. Insomnia, guilt, nausea, flashbacks, irritability…they were her constant bedfellows, not to mention the added bonus of selective amnesia, to top it off. It had taken all her courage and the help of a strong beta-blocker to manage the bustling concourse at Paddington, the noise of which had caused her to break out in a sweat and run for the nearest loo while her body forcibly rejected the memories that rushed forth in a tidal wave. It had taken yet more strength to board the train, dragging two enormous suitcases behind her, and the only reason she'd forced herself to do it was on account of being unable to drive whilst taking anti-depressants. She'd been faced with Hobson's choice: stop taking the medication prescribed by her psychiatrist in order to drive to Cornwall—which was not an option—or face her greatest fear and board a train, instead.

Cornwall.

The enormity of the decision she'd made was enough to elicit a fresh film of sweat.

What had she done?

It had been a rainy morning in April when she'd first seen the advert in *The Bookseller* magazine, which she'd been thumbing through listlessly to rekindle some of the former joy she'd once felt in reading about the latest publishing news. She'd read about her friend, Francesca Ogilvie, taking up her former position as Senior Commissioning Editor at Frenchman Saunders, and about Saffron Wallows signing a new two-book deal with the company as Frenchie's first major acquisition.

She was happy for them both.

After all, she could no longer perform the role she'd once done so well; at the start of the year, her agoraphobia had been so acute that she'd been unable to leave the house, let alone meet with clients or go into the office. Her boss, a woman by the name of Jacinta Huffington-Brown, had been sympathetic but, despite all the cards and flowers, Gabrielle had sensed a lingering doubt as to whether she'd be able to handle the job.

Take a sabbatical, Jacinta had offered. *Go on a nice long holiday.*

But Gabrielle had known things would never be the same, so she'd done the only decent thing, and tendered her resignation.

She'd seen the relief flit across her boss's face, swiftly replaced by an expression of regret.

Well, if you're sure…

Gabrielle smiled, sadly. Once, being a commissioning editor had been all her dreams come true. Now, she could barely find the energy to pick up a book.

That's when she'd seen the advert.

REMOTE BOOKSHOP CAFÉ
SEEKS NEW MANAGER

Carnance Cove Books & Gifts seeks permanent manager, immediate start. £28,500 p.a. inclusive of accommodation, subject to probationary period. Must have extensive knowledge of bookselling and business management, and a friendly, down-to-earth manner. Lovers of sea, sand and scones preferred. Apply directly to Nell...

Whether it was the promise of scones or sandy beaches, she couldn't say, but Gabrielle had fired off an e-mail attaching her CV before she could talk herself out of it, without much hope of any response. Whilst she knew all about books, she'd never worked as a bookseller on the front lines, dealing with the reading public. She'd never grappled with orders and dispatches or difficult customers, so there was no reason she should stand out from the rest of the applicants.

Besides, she'd never so much as set foot in Cornwall before.

Oh, she knew it was beautiful, and had planned to visit long before then, but had never quite found the time. London had a way of stealing your weekends and holidays, and there always seemed to be some 'exotic' foreign adventure Mark had preferred over a UK staycation. But stuck in the confines of her new rental apartment, which held none of the comforts of 'home', life in London seemed stale and lonely. Walking its streets made her feel vulnerable, and using public transport was out of the question.

She'd become a prisoner of her own mind, and it was time to break free.

It had therefore come as both a shock and a delight when she'd received an e-mail a couple of weeks later from the aforementioned 'Nell', inviting her to complete a telephone interview. Despite all her corporate experience, she'd been nervous at the prospect of selling herself to a stranger she'd never met; as if, somehow, despite the physical distance, they'd be able to sense the fear in her voice and know all the secrets of her heart.

For she had chosen not to mention what had happened, stating only that she was ready for a fresh start and a change of pace, working in an area she was passionate about.

That part was true, at least.

In the end, she'd enjoyed the conversation. Nell had a way of drawing her out and making her feel at ease, encouraging her to talk about her life in books and all the authors she'd worked with. When Nell had asked the inevitable question, 'So, Gabi, tell me why you want to move to Cornwall?' she'd found the answer came to her more easily than she'd expected: 'I want to feel the breath of the sea on my face.'

Nell had laughed at that, and warned her that she'd feel more than just the sea's breath during the winter, but still, the answer seemed to have pleased her. Sure enough, the very next day, Gabi received another e-mail, this time inviting her to take up the role at Carnance Cove Books & Gifts for a probationary period, starting as soon as her current notice period ran out and subject to satisfactory references. She'd stared at the offer for all of five minutes before typing an acceptance e-mail, choosing to thrust aside any niggling doubts she might have had about whether she was in the right frame of mind to be making big life decisions so soon after...

After the fall.

She couldn't bring herself to call it an 'attack', because to suffer an attack would necessarily make her the 'victim', which was a word she'd heard far too many times over the course of the past six months—from the police liaison officer at the Metropolitan Police, her family and the people she'd called friends.

Managing a tiny bookshop in a remote Cornish cove wouldn't just be an opportunity to rediscover herself and her love of books—it would be the perfect escape. Sunshine, sandy beaches and idyllic blue waters...

What could go wrong?

CHAPTER 2

For one thing, the weather did not entirely meet Gabrielle's expectation of blue skies and sunbeams.

When she exited the train at Truro Station after an interminably long journey from London, it was late afternoon and the heavens had opened. Rain poured down in sheets, plastering her hair to her head and drenching every item of luggage she owned, which at least served to camouflage the sweat that had beaded her brow while she'd navigated the step from the train onto the platform edge.

Her feet slapped in the gathering puddles as she made her way towards the exit, the pretty tan leather sandals she'd worn offering little protection against what was fast turning into a monsoon.

Puffing from the effort and wishing fervently that she'd packed less in the way of summer dresses and more in the way of cosy jumpers, she paused beneath a canopy overlooking the car park and peered through the rain for any sign of the woman who was supposed to meet her from the train. She saw plenty of men in suits returning home for the weekend, and couples reunited, but there was no sign of Nell Trelawney.

Gabrielle felt an immediate sense of panic.

Closing her eyes, she followed the steps her psychiatrist had coached her to take, counting silently to ten while she breathed in slowly through her nose and exhaled slowly through her mouth.

Nell was probably running a bit late, that was all. No reason to be concerned.

Ten minutes later, when there was still no sign, she began to worry that she'd given her new employer the wrong time and quickly brought up the e-mail on her phone to check. There in black and white, she'd clearly stated that the train would be getting into Truro at seventeen-oh-four.

At a bit of a loss, Gabrielle perched on the edge of one of her suitcases and decided to give it another five minutes before putting a call through to see where she was. In the meantime, she listened to the rain pattering against the glass overhead and watched as the last remaining stragglers from the London train drove away to their respective homes and families.

Summer rain, makes me feel fine…

Gabrielle hummed the old tune while she searched for Nell's telephone number, but looked up when a battered old Land Rover swung into the car park at speed, sloshing water across the tarmac as it went. She narrowed her eyes, trying to make out its driver behind the *swish* of windscreen wipers, but she needn't have bothered.

It certainly wasn't Nell.

The driver was a tall man dressed in a heavy-duty rain jacket and jeans, his feet encased in practical walking boots that were, no doubt, waterproof. She could scarcely make out a face beneath the hood of his jacket, but he carried a lazy, unhurried air despite the inclement weather that she found mildly irritating. Keeping his head ducked against the rain, which was by now coming in sideways, she watched him cross the car park in long strides towards where she sat huddled and bedraggled beneath the canopy. Expecting him to move past her and into the station entrance, she was startled when he came to stand in front of her, his body looming over her like some creature from the deep.

"Gabrielle Adams?"

To her surprise, his accent was not Cornish but pure Irish.

"Yes?"

"Nell sent me to collect you," he said, easily. "She sends her apologies, but she's been delayed."

Gabrielle waited for him to tell her his name and, when it was not forthcoming, asked the obvious question.

"Do you work for Nell?"

He laughed, and the action dislodged his hood, which fell back to reveal an attractive, tanned face and a pair of bright blue eyes that were crinkled at the edges.

"No," he said, unhelpfully. "But she's a friend. Come on, we'd better make tracks—unless you want to sit out here all day?"

Gabrielle gritted her teeth and tried again. "Do I get to know your name? Or is it a secret?"

He reached across to grasp the handle of one of her suitcases, and then the other.

"No secret," he said, flicking another glance in her direction. "I'm Luke."

Just 'Luke', she thought, irritably. *No second name required.*

But good manners prevailed.

"Thank you for coming to collect me," she said.

"Don't mention it," he muttered. Then, without waiting for her to follow him, moved off into the rain again, trailing both suitcases behind him.

Gabrielle could have made a token protest but, to tell the truth, she was glad of the help. The journey had been a long one and, even if it hadn't, the effort it had taken for her to make it this far without breaking down had taken a toll, leaving her feeling drunk with tiredness.

Hiking her handbag on one shoulder and a small rucksack containing her laptop and some other valuables on the other, she gathered up her remaining strength and ran after him.

The car was toasty when Gabrielle clambered inside, and she allowed herself the small, private luxury of relaxing back against the worn leather seat for a few seconds, letting the warm air penetrate her sodden clothes.

Only to be interrupted by the excited bark of a large, golden Labrador, from somewhere over her right shoulder.

She yelped—it was the only way to describe the noise that came forth from her lips—and swung around to find him…her…*it*, staring at her with big, glossy brown eyes and what she could have sworn was a smile on its furry face.

"Gabrielle, meet Madge," Luke said, climbing into the driver's seat beside her.

She noticed he'd removed his outer jacket to reveal a simple cotton shirt, rolled up at the sleeves, and he carried a beach towel in his hands.

"Here," he said, offering it to her. "Thought you might want to dry off a bit."

"Thanks," she said.

He studied her face, noting the dark circles beneath her eyes and the pale skin, which spoke of sleepless nights.

"You don't mind dogs, do you? Sorry, I should have checked, before."

Gabrielle looked back at the Labrador, who had settled herself comfortably on the back seat and was already snoring like a trooper.

"No, I don't mind."

He nodded and started up the engine.

"Why 'Madge'?" she wondered aloud, thinking of a character from *The Simpsons*.

"Short for 'Madonna'," he explained, with the quick flash of a smile. "She's a bit of a diva."

Gabrielle grinned at that. "I wouldn't have pegged you as a fan of hers," she said, and risked another glance at his profile.

"Oh? Don't I look the type?"

"Frankly? No. I'd have put you as more of a fan of Led Zeppelin, or maybe Guns 'n' Roses."

"I'll listen to most things."

He would, she thought. He had a disarming manner she found relaxing, despite herself, and she could imagine many people would find him easy to talk to.

She'd have to be careful.

There was a companionable silence as they wound through the cathedral city of Truro, which was Cornwall's county town, or so Google had informed her. Gabrielle saw little of it through the driving rain before they'd joined the winding, tree-lined road that would take them towards the southernmost tip of the country known as the 'Lizard Peninsula', where Carnance Cove lay nestled amongst the cliffs.

"What brings you to this neck of the woods?" he asked, as they rounded yet another hairpin bend.

Gabrielle gripped the edge of her seat, and tried to appear unaffected.

"Um—I—I wanted a change of scene," she said, and held her breath as the next bend approached. "I was tired of London."

He nodded, and applied his foot to the brake with more care than he might otherwise have done, for which she was eternally grateful.

"During the off-season, it's a quiet life in Carnance," he said. "I hope it won't be too much of a contrast for you."

"Quiet suits me just fine," she said.

Luke thought again of the shadows beneath her eyes, and wondered what it was she was running from.

They were all running from something.

CHAPTER 3

The sun had fallen low in the sky by the time they finally reached the sea.

They'd outrun the rain somewhere past Truro, emerging from its steely-grey curtain to discover the glorious blue skies Gabrielle had dreamed of. They drove against the flow of traffic, passing cars full of early summer tourists who'd enjoyed the beaches without having to share them with hordes of children who would, in a matter of days, be released from the school gates to swarm their golden sands, until winding country lanes flanked by tall, overgrown hedgerows gave way to open farmland and, beyond it, the Atlantic Ocean. Finally, Luke brought the Land Rover to a stop in a car park at the top of the cliffs and turned off the engine, bringing his arms up to rest on the steering wheel.

"There," he said, nodding at the panorama in front of them. "What do you say to that, city girl?"

For a moment, Gabrielle could only stare, drinking in the sight of a sky that seemed to be melting from shades of palest yellow all the way through to deepest ochre as the sun prepared to slip off the edge of the world.

"It looks like it's on fire," she said, reverently.

"The colours are slightly different every night," he said, softly. "It's impossible to capture their exact shade."

Her ears pricked up at that. "Are you an artist?"

"I try to be."

Gabrielle looked at him, then at the sunset, and decided he might just be the most infuriatingly uncommunicative man she'd ever met. Considering some of the characters she'd known over the years, that was saying quite a bit.

Presently, he roused himself again. "Time to go," he said. "Tide'll be coming in soon."

The significance was lost on her. "What does the tide have to do with it?"

Luke frowned. "Didn't Nell mention?"

"Mention what?"

Luke pulled a face and said, "Ah."

Now, she was really worried. "What does 'ah' mean?" she demanded.

"It means, *ah*, Nell didn't tell you that the cove is only accessible at low tide," he said. "The rest of the time it's cut off, and you can only access it via that road even when the tide is out," he said, pointing across to a nondescript-looking wooden gate. "Unless you fancy trying to scale a slippery rock face, of course."

The humour was lost on Gabrielle, who'd heard the words 'cut off' and nothing much afterwards. "What do you mean by that?" she asked him, and felt a pounding begin to throb in the base of her skull. "You mean, there's only one way in and out—and, even then, it's not always possible?"

"Bingo," he said, and opened the back door to allow Madge to jump out and stretch. "Then again, you said you didn't mind the quiet."

"Quiet is one thing, but this…this is…" She trailed off, realising suddenly that she couldn't even see the cove. In fact, from their clifftop position, all she could see was the car park where they stood and a strip of sea merging with the horizon.

"Why don't you come down and take a look, before you hurry back to London?" he said, reading her mind. "You wouldn't be the only person living down at Carnance—it has a standing population of five—six, if you decide to stay."

"*Five?*"

"Well, there's yours truly, Nell and her son, Jackson, and old Jude Barker and his wife, Pat. Now, I guess if you're counting pets, that would make"—he paused to do the mental arithmetic—"nine, including dogs and cats."

"I bet you think this is hilarious."

"The look on your face is priceless," he admitted, and popped the boot to lift out her bags once more. "You look as if you've stumbled into Narnia."

"It feels like it," she said, weakly.

"Come on," he said. "We may not find Mr Tumnus, but with the light falling just as it is, you might find that rainbow you've been looking for, Uptown Girl."

"So you've moved from Madonna to Billy Joel, now?"

"I have a wide repertoire," he threw back over his shoulder, and began whistling the tune as he made for the plain wooden gate that led down to another world.

Gabrielle followed Luke down a meandering pathway for a quarter of a mile before catching her first sight of Carnance Cove and, when she did, it took her breath away.

The path gave way to soft sand that was still warm underfoot and she kicked off her sandals so that she could wriggle her toes between the soft grains. A golden yellow beach spread out before them, curving around a short headland and between a number of smaller stacked outcrops of rock which, she imagined, would be inaccessible at high tide unless one was prepared to swim. Perfectly clean, turquoise-blue water lapped gently at the shoreline, edging ever closer as the tide drew in for the evening. Madge ran on ahead with a cheery bark, obviously well familiar with the route, and as Gabrielle watched its lithe body bounding through the shallows, she found herself envying the animal its uncomplicated freedom.

As they rounded the headland, the beach spread out into a sheltered cove where a cluster of small cottages had been built on higher ground above the waterline. On the near side was what she guessed to be the bookshop and café, which jutted out on a long plateau that benefited from a terraced area upon which a few pretty tables and chairs had been laid out, their parasols now closed for the day. Nearby, there was a line of three stone fishermen's cottages, all painted in white with royal blue window trims, as was customary in the area. Another cottage lay on the far side of the cove, and had been modified to include an impressive glass extension that would give its owner unrivalled views across the sea.

Aside from a couple of little boats and a wooden structure upon which had been painted, 'THE SURF SHACK', that was about it.

Luke had paused to allow her to catch up, and she was reminded that he'd carried her bulky suitcases across the sand for quite a distance without so much as a murmur of complaint.

Mark would never have done that, came the unbidden thought.

"Thank you so much for helping me with the bags," she said, in a bit of a rush.

He shrugged, and then rolled out his shoulders.

"I'm hoping they won't need to make a return journey any time soon," he said, and flashed her one of his smiles. "What do you think of Carnance?"

Gabrielle turned to look again at the water, which glistened like a jewel in the evening sunlight, then down at the sand beneath her feet.

"It's paradise," she said simply.

CHAPTER 4

Carnance Cove Books & Gifts was another slice of heaven, as far as Gabrielle was concerned.

Consisting of a long single-storey structure with one large, open-plan space, there was a service counter at one end of the building spanning almost its entire width, half dedicated to a chilled unit displaying cakes and pastries of the day and half featuring selected books of the week and an area for bagging and payment. The middle portion of the room was dedicated to books, with tall shelving on the side walls and shorter bookshelves covering the space in between, so as not to block out the light. At the far end facing the sea there was a large seating area with double doors leading onto the terrace Gabrielle had spotted on the way in, with floor-to-ceiling glass windows to allow diners to sit and watch the world go by. Craning her neck, she noticed what appeared to be a children's corner where miniature tables and chairs had been set up with paper and pencils, as well as a selection of well-thumbed books which the shop had made available to those who were not in a position to buy.

Nice touch, Gabrielle thought.

A commercial decision too, no doubt. After all, the parents of said children would be more likely to stay longer and pay for coffee and a sandwich while their kids were happily entertained.

"Bloody buggering hell!"

There followed a long stream of well-chosen expletives that might have made a pirate blush, then Nell Trelawney appeared in the doorway leading to the kitchen and back office with a face like thunder. Gabrielle's first impression was of a stocky, well-built woman who seemed to be possessed of both generous curves as well as brute strength, which could be a dangerous combination. Her skin was tanned a deep chestnut brown and her hair, which had been left to go grey, curled in a halo around a remarkably unlined face that had been accentuated with blue eyeliner and bright pink lipstick. Giant gold hoops hung from her ears, while all of her fingers except one were covered in silver rings of all shapes and size. She wore faded jean cut-offs and a baggy pink jumper that slipped over one shoulder, and her feet rested comfortably in well-worn banana yellow flip-flops, giving the overall impression of a modern-day buccaneer. While standards of the age would not have deemed her beautiful, Nell was arresting at the very least, and her presence commanded attention.

"The soddin' dishwasher's on the blink again," she declared, wiping her hands on a mucky tea towel. "I've had that no-good Hector Treen out to fix it twice now, and it's still leakin' all o'er my floor. I wouldn't care, but the blasted thing's only six months old."

"I'll take a look at it," Luke said, and promptly made his way through the doorway into the kitchen.

"Nothing's ever too much trouble for that one," Nell said happily, with a wink for Gabrielle that said clearly that she'd hoped Luke would offer to lend a hand.

She set the tea towel on the counter and then moved around it to take a better look at her new employee. As she did, Madge nosed her way through the open door of the café and came to sit beside her, shoving its muzzle into her hand.

Nell obliged, and gave the dog a good scratch on the crown of its head.

"Well now, you must be my new manager, all the way from London," she said.

"Pleased to meet you, Mrs Trelawney," Gabrielle said formally, and stuck out her hand.

Nell looked at it, tried to remember the last time she'd needed to shake anybody's hand, and couldn't. All the same, she took the woman's fingers in her own and gave them a reassuring squeeze.

"Please, call me Nell. Most folks do."

"Thank you," Gabi murmured.

"And are you a 'Gabrielle', 'Gabi', 'Miss Adams'…or, 'Ms'?" she tagged on.

"Gabrielle or Gabi, either is fine by me."

Nell smiled, but her sharp eyes noted in the strain the girl was obviously trying to hide, and the slight tremble she'd felt as she'd held her hand.

"You must be exhausted, after the journey you've had," she said kindly. "There's plenty of time to look around here tomorrow—why don't I show you where you'll be staying, so you can get settled in?"

"Thank you," Gabrielle said.

"Get you somethin' to eat, too," Nell continued, as she made a grab for one of the suitcases. "There's not a pickin' on you, but that'll change after you've lived here for a while and sampled some of Pat's cooking."

Gabrielle remembered Luke saying something about there being an old couple, Jude and Pat Barker.

"Does Pat work for you?"

Nell smiled, and held open the door for Gabi to precede her outside with the other suitcase.

"She does all the baking for the café here," Nell explained. "Has done for the past twenty years. Jude helps with most other things hereabouts."

She led Gabrielle along a well-tended stone pathway towards the row of fishermen's cottages she'd seen from the beach.

"They have the end cottage, Number 1," she continued, jutting her chin towards the first in the row. "Middle one's vacant at the moment; I usually let it out to tourists in the high season. End one's yours."

Gabrielle smiled, taking in the charming image of the little stone cottage with its garland of pink roses trailing over a wooden half-canopy above the front door, and could hardly believe her good fortune.

"I suppose the cottage further up the hill there, with the glass conservatory, must be Luke's?"

But Nell shook her head.

"That'd be mine," she said. "Me and my son, Jackson, live there—when he cares to, that is."

The last comment was spoken with a degree of indulgence, and Gabrielle found herself wanting to find out more about this woman and her family. There had been no mention of a 'Mr Trelawney', and she was too polite to enquire.

That didn't stop her asking another question, however.

"If that one's yours, where does Luke live? I thought he said that he had a place here in Carnance?"

Nell nodded.

"So he does. Luke built himself a nice place further up the hill," she said, and paused outside Gabrielle's new front door to point towards another pathway Gabrielle hadn't noticed before, which wound around the back of the cottages. Tipping her head up, she saw a glass and wooden structure tucked into the side of the cliff, well designed so as not to be obtrusive, whilst still affording what must have been a spectacular view of the cove.

"I wonder how he managed to get permission to build it," Gabrielle wondered aloud.

"Perhaps he sweet-talked the landowner," Nell said, with a twinkle in her eye. "Now, where did I put the key…ah, here we are."

Belatedly, Gabrielle thought back to what Nell had said about renting out the middle cottage…and then about the bookshop and café.

"Do you...um, do you own all these buildings, then?"

"Yup," Nell said, and stuck a key in the lock of the third cottage. "I bought this little cove and everything in it thirty years ago, when I came into some money."

Gabrielle told herself it was rude to stare, or to allow one's jaw to drop, but it took all the willpower she possessed.

"You're wondering what in the name of Blackbeard's Ghost I could have done to afford to buy this place, lock, stock 'n' barrel, aren't you?" Nell said, with a knowing chuckle. "Well, there's no shame in being curious, and it's no secret—I won the lottery, back when it was worth winning."

Gabrielle couldn't hide her surprise.

"I know, I know," Nell said, sagely. "You're thinking that, with this face and figure, I might have bagged myself some rich old man who'd left me all his gold, eh?"

She let out a bawdy chuckle, which elicited a smile from Gabrielle in return.

"The truth is, I was twenty-two, without a penny to my name," she said openly, and gestured for Gabi to go inside. "I'd had Jackson three months before and, I don't mind telling you, I was worried sick about how I was going to provide for us both. His father wasn't in the picture anymore, and my family aren't much to speak of. I'd never normally put the lottery on, so I don't rightly know why I ended up spending a pound I could scarce afford…desperation, probably," she muttered. "Whatever the reason, it paid off and I was able to cover my leccy bill after all."

Nudging the front door closed again, she flicked on the lights in the little hallway.

"Well, here we are," she declared. "I hope this'll do."

The cottage was by no means large, but it had all that Gabrielle would ever need. Beyond the narrow, white-washed hallway with its driftwood-framed images of sailing boats and sunsets, there was a cosy sitting room with a log-burning fire and an enormous, overstuffed couch with a window facing out to sea. At the back of the cottage was a kitchen-diner with good quality wooden units and seating for four, a small wash-cloakroom, and a back door leading outside to a tiny courtyard. A narrow staircase led from the hallway upstairs, where there was a master bedroom with a tiny shower room, a small second bedroom and a larger bathroom with a claw-tubbed bath.

"It's wonderful," Gabrielle said, and meant it. When she'd imagined the accommodation that might come with her job package, she'd thought of a poky, run-down flat or something of that kind, but had never dared to dream of anything so generous.

"Hope the commute to work won't be too much for you?" Nell joked.

Gabrielle estimated the steps between the cottage and the bookshop to be no more than fifty, door-to-door.

She pulled an expressive face. "I'll have to manage, somehow..."

Nell let out another throaty laugh. "You'll do," she said, and pointed to the fridge in the kitchen. "There's supplies in there to keep you going for now. Anything else you need, you can get from Luddo, which is the nearest village to here—no more'n a five-minute drive."

A shadow passed over Gabrielle's face, for she was still unable to drive thanks to the strong medication she'd been prescribed.

Nell must have picked up on the sudden change in mood.

"Perhaps you haven't sorted out a car, yet?" she said. "Never mind. You can get most provisions at the bookshop, because we've got daily deliveries coming in for milk, bread…whatever you like, really. Let me know, and I'll add it to the order."

Gabrielle visibly relaxed.

"Thank you," she said, and realised she was beginning to sound like a parrot. There just seemed to be so much to thank this woman for; more than she could ever know.

"I'll leave you to it," Nell said, with an eye for the time, and turned to leave.

Then, turned back again, snapping her fingers as she remembered something.

"I'm doing a bit of dinner at my place tomorrow night, around seven. Thought you might like to come along and meet your new neighbours, such as they are?"

Gabrielle thought of how little she'd socialised over the past six months, and worried if she'd be able to remember how it was done.

"I'd like that," she said, and tried to inject the requisite enthusiasm into her voice.

"Good. You don't need to start work till Monday, but why not pop round to the bookshop tomorrow morning and get the lay of the land? I'll introduce you to the Saturday team, who help us with the serving and the fetching."

"I'll be there," Gabrielle promised her.

"I'll say 'goodnight' then," Nell replied, and made to leave.

"Um—Nell?"

"Yes, love?"

"Can I have the key, please?"

Nell looked confused for a moment, then her face cleared.

"It's so rare for people to lock their doors around here, I nearly forgot," she said, and dropped the door key into Gabrielle's waiting palm. "Anything else you need, just shout."

Gabrielle waited until Nell had walked a few feet from the cottage, then locked and bolted the door behind her. Remote cove or not, her demons followed her wherever she went, and there would be no way of sleeping that night unless she could be sure that all the doors and windows were secured.

It was the price she paid for paradise.

CHAPTER 5

The air rushed out of Gabrielle's body in one long, silent scream.

She felt herself falling, fingers grasping at nothing but air as her body plunged into oblivion, and she was powerless to stop it.

Help...help me, please!

But no sound could be heard above the piercing screech of the train's brakes, the roar of its horn warning her to *move!*

Move now!

Heart pounding, the air coming in short gasps through her chest, she waited for death, staring mutely up at those who watched her from above, their faces unmoving and impassive.

She's a paranoid mess, Mark said to the others. *I told her, she should wash her hair.*

I'll write about this, Geoffrey told him. *It'll be the next big thing, you'll see.*

I'd love to stick around, Frenchie said. *But I have other plans.*

It sends a higher message, Saffron said. *It's for the best.*

We'll miss you, Jacinta mouthed, and they began to move away, one by one, their faces disappearing into the murky shadows of the train station.

Come back!

Please, come back!

The train was almost upon her now, and she was paralysed.

Mind the gap…

Gabrielle awoke in a film of clammy sweat, mouth wide open as she dragged great, gulping breaths of oxygen into her lungs.

For a terrible moment, she thought she was really paralysed, but it was merely that her legs had become entangled with the duvet cover some time during the course of her nightmare. With unsteady hands, she freed herself, then dragged her legs up to her chest to lie in the foetal position while thin, early morning sunlight streamed through her bedroom window.

Her dreams were always very similar. In the first few months after the fall, her psychiatrist had encouraged her to keep a journal, so she would remember the details and be able to deconstruct their meaning at some later date. But it wasn't the dreams she had difficulty remembering, or the horror of falling onto the tracks, it was everything else from that night.

Sometimes, small wisps of a memory would materialise, and she tried to grasp it before it evaporated again and left her with the frustration of knowing the remnants existed somewhere in her brain, behind a locked door to which she had lost the key.

It was a major stumbling block for the police, she knew that much.

When they'd come to interview her at the hospital, their new star witness—the *only* living witness to survive an attack from The Tube Killer—they had high hopes she'd be able to give them a blow-by-blow account of her ordeal and a handy description of her assailant.

She wanted to help them, but she couldn't.

No matter how hard she tried, she could not recall the hours prior to the fall, and her movements immediately following her rescue were patchy as well. All she knew of it was what others had told her, and what had been widely reported in the news: that she'd been pushed onto the tracks of an oncoming train at South Kensington station in the early hours of a December morning, by a person or persons unknown. She'd managed to survive only by a quirk of fate: the ground where she'd fallen having been hollowed out sufficiently deep following some work to the drains in that area, to allow her body to dip beneath the level of the train.

A few inches either way and she would have been pulped.

Her stomach rolled, and she hurried from the bed to the adjoining shower room, where she heaved up the remains of a tuna sandwich she'd made the evening before, in lieu of a proper dinner.

When there was nothing left but bile, she braced her hands on the sink and looked at herself in the small cabinet mirror above.

Her eyes bore a haunted expression, which was hardly surprising. There were dark purple shadows beneath them, and her cheeks were hollowed out, probably since she'd lost her appetite, as well as over two stone in weight since the beginning of the year.

She hadn't exactly been curvy to begin with.

Have you ever thought of getting a boob job, Gabi? Mark had once asked her, while they'd been sunbathing on a beach in Greece. *You'd look great, as a C- or a D-cup. If it's the money holding you back, I could help out...*

She hadn't sunbathed again, after that.

A sudden cramp in her leg drove the old memory away, replacing it with a more urgent need to sit down and rub the pain away. Never one to suffer from cramp before, it was another new staple in her life, and tended to concentrate itself around her calf, near the site where she'd broken her right tibia after it had taken the brunt of her landing on the train tracks.

Rooting around for her daily pills, Gabrielle knocked them back with a glass of water and then limped through the bedroom towards the window, where she pulled back the blinds. The sight of the sea brushing against the harbour wall, and of the misty, lilac-blue skies overhead, was enough to banish any self-pity from her heart, which soared at the picture-perfect pairing of man and nature. The cramp in her leg momentarily forgotten, she leaned against the window frame and watched the morning awaken, feeling at peace for a few precious moments.

A movement in her peripheral vision broke the picture postcard, reminding her that she did not have the cove to herself, after all. She caught sight of a tall man in a summer wetsuit, half undone to the waist, making his way down the pathway leading from Nell's place towards the little harbour. He passed beneath her bedroom window with a paddleboard tucked underneath his arm and, for a moment, she thought he might have been Luke—but this man's hair was lighter, his skin tanned the same shade as his mother's.

Jackson Trelawney.

She watched him make his way down to the harbour wall, where the sea that had drawn in sometime during the night was now beginning to retreat again, leaving a shallow area of pebble-dashed sand that would eventually give way to the wide golden sands of yesterday. He paused there to check his gear and shrug into the rest of his wetsuit, then pushed off onto the water with powerful arms.

In the privacy of her own room, Gabrielle could admit that, so far, Cornwall had more than merely sunshine, sand and a quaint bookshop to recommend it.

CHAPTER 6

Gabrielle spent a pleasant hour unpacking the remainder of her suitcases, and made a list of household items she needed to pick up—though where she would get them, she had no idea. Without her own wheels and with her immediate options limited to baked goods, ice cream or books, the solution did not immediately present itself.

Amazon?

They delivered everywhere, didn't they? Why not a tiny cove with tidal access?

Amused by the prospect, she hunted out her mobile phone, intending to call up the website to see if they covered her postcode, only to find there was zero mobile reception.

"Hmm," she murmured, though she was hardly surprised.

Nell had mentioned something about there being patchy Wi-Fi, so she went off in search of the router. After entering the requisite twelve-digit code for 'Carnance Wifi', she waited expectantly for the search engine to respond accordingly.

And was met with a grey screen and a polite message telling her, in computer speak, to dream on.

Feeling stumped, she looked around the kitchen and the living room, opening cupboards here and there in search of an ordinary telephone, but found none.

How was she supposed to stay in touch with the outside world?

Gabrielle left the cottage shortly after nine-thirty to walk the short distance to the bookshop, which was now open to the public. From the window in her sitting room, she'd watched the tide pull back far enough to allow access from the car park further around the headland and, as soon as it had, they began to arrive in their droves: men, women and young children armed with all manner of beach paraphernalia, ready to spend a day shell-seeking and sunbathing.

But she'd barely taken a couple of steps before she was forced to turn back, the familiar pummelling in her chest just too pressing to ignore.

Tears of humiliation burned the back of her eyes, but Gabrielle followed the compulsion, her fingers reaching out to check the lock on the door.

Once...

Twice...

A third time.

Angry at herself, but needing to be sure, she trailed around the side of the cottage to check the back door, as well.

Once...

Twice...

A third time.

Cupping her hands to peer through the kitchen window, she could see everything was just as she'd left it, with one of the kitchen chairs still propped against the back door to provide further protection against any intruders.

"Forgotten your key, lovie?"

Gabrielle let out a startled cry, and spun back against the door to find a woman of around seventy or thereabouts smiling amiably at her from across the low stone wall that separated their cottages.

Pat Barker, she surmised.

"N—no, thank you," Gabi stammered, and left it at that.

"Because, you know, Nell always keeps a spare in her lock box," Pat continued. "Just in case you lose it in the sand. Wouldn't be the first time somebody's done that!"

"No, I suppose not," Gabrielle said, lamely.

"You must be the girl from London," Pat said, resting her arms on the wall to settle in for a natter. "Nell told us you'd come from one of the big publishing houses there."

"Yes, that's right."

"Must be a bit of a change for you," she remarked, and the breath-taking understatement of it all brought a smile to Gabi's lips.

"You could say that," she agreed. "Everyone's been very kind, so far, considering—"

"You're from 'Up Country'?" Pat finished for her, and then laughed. "I was born in Birmingham, myself—many moons ago now, of course. Met my Jude while I was down here with some friends for a little holiday, and I never went back."

"That sounds romantic," Gabrielle said.

"He's a handy man, my Jude," the woman said, enigmatically. "Be seein' you."

With that, she sent Gabrielle a cheery wave and ducked back inside her own cottage, leaving the latter to wonder whether she'd been referring to Jude's prowess with a hammer and nails, or something else entirely.

There must be something in the air...

CHAPTER 7

The bookshop was bustling with people by the time Gabrielle pushed through its jingling doorway at a quarter to ten. Most of the tables were already full, and there was a queue of people waiting for service at the counter.

"Beep beep!" Nell said, and Gabi stepped out of the way to allow her to bustle past with two platefuls of what appeared to be eggs benedict.

"Where did all these people come from?" she asked, when her employer made the return journey.

"Here, there, and everywhere," came the response. "Come on back, and I'll give you the whistle-stop tour. Amy!"

Nell paused to call across to a girl who had been restocking a shelf full of small 'pocket money' gifts for children.

"Take over food service for a minute, would you?"

Gabrielle smiled at a shy but able-looking girl of around seventeen, exchanged a polite 'hello' and then followed Nell's retreating back, which was dressed in denim dungarees embroidered with 'PEACHY' on the rear end.

"Back here's the kitchen," she was saying, as they dipped behind the counter and through a swing door.

And what a kitchen it was.

If Gabrielle had expected a couple of Formica countertops with a microwave and perhaps a bog-standard oven, she was sorely mistaken. Instead, she saw a compact but well-equipped space, with plenty of stainless steel and a professional baker's oven. A large print on the wall read, 'WORK HARD AND BE KIND TO PEOPLE', beneath which had been tacked a number of photographs featuring Nell with her staff, all of them smiling.

"That's the leavers' wall," she explained. "A lot of our staff are seasonal, so they come and do a summer before they head off to university, or whatever it might be. It's nice to remember their faces."

Gabrielle nodded, and wondered whether there was a single photograph of her gracing the fridge in the break room at Frenchman Saunders.

Probably not.

"So, as you can see, this is where the magic happens," Nell said, spreading her arms to encompass the kitchen. "I don't expect you to roll up your sleeves and start making sandwiches, because I've got plenty of people for that. Pat does our baking, Amy and Elena come and help with the serving, and I do any other cooking that's required."

Gabrielle was surprised.

"I enjoy it." Nell answered her unspoken question. "Keeps me out of mischief. Does no good for a person to be idle, no matter how many lotteries they've won. The devil makes work for idle hands, doesn't he? Now, through here…"

She led Gabrielle through the kitchen to a door marked, 'PRIVATE', and pushed it open to reveal a large storeroom lined with industrial metal shelving, upon which had been stacked books of all genres but particularly children's stories, romantic-looking escapades set by the sea, and cookery books featuring bearded men holding freshly-caught fish on the front cover.

"We cater for the crowd," Nell said, with a self-deprecating shrug. "There was a time when I had high hopes of selling books of all kinds in this little place but, for some strange reason, people don't turn to *Ulysses* while they're relaxing on the beach."

Gabrielle chuckled.

"Here's the office area," Nell continued, gesturing to a large desk with monitor and printer, overshadowed by a pin board full of little reminder notes. "I'll clear it out a bit, but this'll be your domain from now on. I have my own office at home."

Nell leaned back against the desktop and gave her a direct look.

"Fact is, Gabi, I've been doing too much, lately. My age is startin' to catch up with me."

She held up a hand before Gabrielle could speak.

"I know, I know...I barely look a day over thirty," she said, with a wink. "I've been trying to run the café as well as the bookshop, but they've both grown so quickly, I'm starting to do neither of those things very well. That's where you come in."

Gabrielle was all ears.

"It may not seem like much, but people come from miles around to browse the shelves in here and thumb through the pages of *Jane Eyre* while their kids are having a paddle-board lesson," Nell said. "Now and then, we run an old folks reading group, where one of us takes a selection of stories to a local care home or hospital wing and we read to the elderly. When we've run events here in the past, we've seen the same faces turn out—regulars, you might say—and they're the people who've lost loved ones and need to feel part of something, with people who share the same interests. Do you know what I'm trying to say?"

"I think so," she replied. "You're telling me, Carnance Books is more than just a bookshop. It's a community hub, and a lifeline for some people."

Nell nodded, pleased that she understood.

"I'm asking you to tread a funny, wiggly sort of line, Gabi, between turning a profit and continuing to build a business whose fundamental ethos doesn't centre around money. It'll feel strange, coming from somewhere like Frenchman Saunders."

"It'll feel refreshing," Gabi corrected her, and was already imagining the things she could do.

Nell nodded, and went on to run through some more of the 'back office' technicalities.

"How does that sound?"

Not half as bad as she'd feared, Gabi thought.

"It sounds like you've got a well-run operation here," she said, honestly. "But there's room for me to help you grow, too. Maybe some author talks, children's events, giveaways, book tours…you never know, maybe we'll convince people to give *Ulysses* a try, after all."

Nell laughed. "I like your attitude," she said. "Anything you need, any questions at all, you know where to find me."

"Well, there is one thing," Gabi said. "A telephone, or at least some sort of signal to the outside world. The Wi-Fi seems patchy, I couldn't get a mobile signal, and there doesn't seem to be any landline at the cottage…"

"Oh, no, there wouldn't be," Nell laughed.

Of course not, Gabi thought, and felt her stomach plummet.

"The Wi-Fi is a lot more reliable here at the shop," Nell went on to say. "If you need to send a personal e-mail, don't worry about using the network here. So long as you're not planning to download anything naughty, I won't mind."

She gave an expressive wriggle of her eyebrows, and Gabi felt a gurgle of laughter rise up, taking her by surprise.

"I'll try not to," she said, deadpan.

"As for mobile reception, there isn't a single bar until you get up to Luke's place, or back up to the car park," Nell said. "You can make a Wi-Fi call from the office here, usually, but if you ever need to make an emergency call, there's an SOS telephone on the beach, beside the harbour wall."

Something of her disquiet must have shown on Gabrielle's face, because Nell gave her a considering look.

"You know, when we spoke before, you said that you wanted a change," she said, carefully. "Most people who find themselves in a place like Carnance have come for the same reason. You've got the look of someone who's carrying a hurt around with you—"

Gabi opened her mouth to deny it, but the lie just wouldn't come.

"—I know, because I had that same look, once upon a time," Nell continued. "Your business is your business but, all I'll say is, this place might feel lonely when the tide comes in but you're never alone. Remember that. You come and knock on my door any time."

Gabi felt a lump rise to her throat, and was embarrassed. Her own mother hadn't so much as bothered to fly back from Marbella to see her, and yet, here was this woman—little more than a stranger, really—offering to be her friend.

"I'll remember," she said, quietly. "Thanks, Nell."

"Well," the other woman said, decisively. "Best put our best feet forward, eh? I'll see you on Monday—"

"Oh, but...that is, it looks as though you could use an extra pair of hands," Gabi said softly. "Why don't I start now?"

Nell favoured her with a beaming smile.

"I can tell we're going to get along just fine. Grab yourself an apron, and muck in."

CHAPTER 8

The rest of the morning passed in a whirlwind, and Gabrielle found herself too busy to feel any more anxiety about the lack of any direct line to the outside world. Indeed, the outside world seemed to have decamped *en masse* to Carnance, and every one of them had been hungry for breakfast, brunch or lunch. The experience had been a whistle-stop training exercise, and she'd gained a number of new skills in the space of only a few hours, including how to use a till, how to serve soft scoop ice-cream without overbalancing the cone and, perhaps most importantly, how to distinguish which customers might be more likely to buy a copy of Winston Graham's *Poldark* series, versus those who would be more in the line for Rick Stein's latest culinary adventure.

Her mind full of requests for ketchup and ideas for cooking demonstrations, she almost dropped the plate she was holding when a warm hand brushed her bare arm.

"I've been sent to relieve you."

Gabrielle turned to find herself looking into a pair of big brown eyes, framed by a chiselled face and over-long light brown hair, liberally streaked with blonde, thanks to hours spent working in the sun. They belonged to the man she'd seen heading out to paddleboard earlier that morning, but, this time, he'd changed into a pair of board shorts and a bright blue t-shirt that featured, 'THE SURF SHACK' in bold lettering on the front. He could have been anywhere between the ages of twenty-five and thirty-five, and she suspected he'd stay that way until he was much older.

"You must be Jackson," she said.

He gave her a slow smile, revealing a set of pearly white teeth.

"That's right," he said. "Does my reputation precede me?"

"I didn't know you had one," she shot back. "But you do look a lot like your mother."

"I'll take that as a compliment," he said. "Speaking of the devil, she says you're to take a break for lunch. Help yourself to anything you like from the kitchen."

Gabrielle hadn't thought she was especially hungry, then her stomach gave a loud rumble.

"I suppose I should eat something," she muttered.

"You should try one of Pat's fruit scones," he said, even while his eyes strayed somewhere over her right shoulder. Turning, Gabi watched Amy hurry into the room with a loaded tray, pause to take a long swig of water, before piling a load of glasses into the dishwasher. The action stretched the material of the girl's shorts, and Gabi turned back to find Jackson prying his eyes away, with obvious reluctance.

"I could join you for a picnic on the beach?" he prodded.

"Don't you have work to do?"

"It's my lunchtime, too," he said, and leaned against the wall to favour her with his best smile. "So, what do you say? I could show you some of the caves—they go back for miles, winding all the way through the cliffs. You and I could get lost in there."

"Tempting, but I want to make a couple of calls. Maybe another time."

"I could—"

"I told you to pass on a message, Jack, not harass the poor girl," Nell scolded him, as she swung into the kitchen. "Go and pester one of those beach bunnies I saw hanging around the Shack."

He sent his mother a pained expression.

"Ma—"

"Skedaddle," she snapped.

With a final, easy smile for Gabrielle, he sauntered out again. As the door swung shut behind him, Nell planted her fists on her hips and shook her head with an air of long sufferance.

"He's a good boy," she said clearly, in a tone that brooked no argument. "Works hard, looks after his old mum, and wouldn't harm a fly. But, when it comes to the opposite sex…well, I might as well tell you, he's the spitting double of his father. A good-looking charmer, who knows how to get what he wants when he sees a pretty girl."

Gabrielle didn't know how to respond, especially to the implication that she was one such 'pretty girl', so fell back on a polite silence while she washed her hands in the sink.

"I can say all this, because I'm his mother," Nell went on. "And, Lord knows, you're a grown woman who can make her own decisions. That being said, don't say you weren't warned. He's got a lot of sowing of wild oats to do, before he'll be ready to settle down—there's a few who've learned that the hard way. Nice girls, too," she added, sadly.

"I'm not on the look-out," Gabi said, to put the woman's mind at ease. "I was—"

Engaged, heart-broken, she almost said.

"—ah, I was recently in a long-term relationship," she amended. "It didn't work out."

Nell clucked her tongue, watching the play of emotions crossing the other woman's face.

"His loss, I'll bet."

Gabi smiled weakly, but wondered if Mark hadn't made a lucky escape. She hadn't been easy to live with, after the fall, what with all the nightmares and episodes...

That was no reason to sleep with another woman, her mind whispered.

She had no idea who that other woman might have been and, really, she had no interest in knowing. Mark had told her there was someone else—had been for a while—and he'd waited long enough for her to recover so that he could leave with a clear conscience. She should be grateful for that much consideration, she supposed.

Gabi scrubbed at her hands with a little more force than was necessary, took her time re-folding the towel, then started the process all over again, hardly aware that she was reaching for the soap or humming the same tune as before.

"Hands still dirty?" Nell asked, with a slight frown.

Gabrielle froze, staring at the running water while her mind scrambled for something to say.

"Oh!" She gave a little laugh. "I must be on auto-pilot, or something."

She forced her fingers to turn off the tap, and told herself she would need to be more careful to try to manage her compulsive habits, in future. Obsessive Compulsive Disorder was just another acronym to add to her burgeoning pile of mental disorders and, with the help of Doctor Gregory, she was working her way through them.

"Ah, I'll take a few minutes for lunch now, if that's all right? I thought I might take a sandwich and explore the cove, a bit," she said, to forestall any pertinent questions that might have been forthcoming.

Nell nodded. "Course, lovie. Enjoy the sunshine—you're looking a bit pale. If you're heading out, would you mind dropping off Luke's lunch order?" She reached inside one of the large fridges for a paper bag containing various goodies, and a bottle of ginger beer, which she handed to her.

"Sure," Gabi said, untying her apron.

"Oh, and this is for Madge." Nell wrapped a giant ham bone in cellophane and rested it beside the bag.

"She's a lady of refined tastes, just like me," she said, and gave one of her bawdy laughs. "Careful on the pathway, mind. It can be slippery, and I wouldn't want you to fall."

A tremor racked Gabrielle's body, and she searched the woman's face for any sign that she *knew*, or that her remark had been deliberate, but saw only the bland, friendly face of one who had made an idle remark.

"I'll be careful," she said, softly.

She was always careful, these days.

CHAPTER 9

As Gabi made her way up the steep, winding incline that led to Luke's property, armed with two paper bags, two bottles of ginger beer and an enormous ham bone, she found herself growing increasingly agitated. It might have been the sun, which beat its merciless rays upon her back, or it could have been the fact that the detour was eating into her lunch time, when she'd planned to go up to the car park and make some calls to family and friends back in London.

But it wasn't either of those things.

It was the simple fact that, despite living so near, His Royal Highness was apparently unable to venture the short distance from his home to collect his own damn lunch order. Oh no, it was left to skivvies like her to pant up the hill on legs that were already shaky and feet that were already aching after a full morning spent pounding the tiled floor of Carnance Books & Gifts.

"Bloody typical," she muttered to herself, between puffs. "He'd better be at home, that's all I can say…"

"He's at home," came a disembodied voice, and she almost jumped.

"Luke?"

"The very same," he replied, and stepped out from behind a giant fern.

So wrapped up had she been in her own, less-than-charitable thoughts, Gabi hadn't realised she'd climbed almost to the top of the path. Much of it was lined with tufted grass and flowering perennials, which sprouted from the underside of the rock face, but, as the land plateaued, it gave way to an unexpected expanse of lush, semi-tropical gardens.

"I didn't see you hiding there," she mumbled, feeling hot and bothered.

His lips twitched.

"Hardly hiding," he said, enjoying the unexpected fire in his new neighbour's eyes. "I was working."

She tried to peer behind the foliage, but could find no clue as to his occupation.

"You were gardening?" she ventured.

Luke smiled, and shook his head before reaching out to pluck the bags from her hands.

"I find it relaxing, as a general rule, but no. I haven't done any gardening today."

He paused, wondering whether to vex her curiosity further by leaving it at that, but even he wasn't so cruel.

"Why don't you come and see for yourself?"

It was on the tip of her tongue to refuse, on principle—whatever that principle might have been—but he didn't wait for her to come up with any bland excuses and simply turned to lead the way.

"Just for a minute," she said quickly. "I have to be back at the shop—"

She half-turned to gesture back down the pathway, and immediately realised her error. Nausea hit her like a punch to the gut, and she swayed on her feet, the ground spinning in front of her.

Hearing the shift in her tone, Luke turned in the nick of time and, dropping the bags without another thought, hurried back to clasp her in his arms.

"Easy there," he said, and turned her away from the view back down the hill. "Look at me. That's right. Just focus on my nose, and see if you can count the freckles."

The notion was so ridiculous, she managed a wan sort of chuckle, even as nausea continued to wash over her in relentless waves.

"You don't have any freckles," she mumbled.

"They're there, if you look closely," he argued, and was pleased to see a touch of colour return to her cheeks. "Let's find you somewhere to sit in the shade."

He led her into his garden and, when she was in full possession of her faculties again, she would think that the setting was glorious. A white, timber-framed, 'New England' style cottage had been built with a long two-storey veranda overlooking the sea and a wide, semi-circular lawn edged with palm trees, rhododendrons and all manner of glossy green plants. The central portion had been cut low so as not to interfere with the view, which was staggering, but he bypassed that and led her towards a bistro table and chairs arranged on a terraced area beneath the shade of a pergola trailing with vines and other topiary.

"Sit here," he said, and plonked her down into one of the chairs before dropping onto his haunches so he could look at her face. "How are you feeling now?"

"Bit better," she managed, keeping her eyes closed while she focused on taking deep breaths in through her nose and breathing out through her mouth. "Sorry for the theatricals."

"I'd love to say that women regularly swoon after seeing me, but you'd be the first," he said.

Unlikely, came the unbidden thought to her mind. As she'd observed the previous day, Luke was a dangerous man to know, and could disarm a woman in such a way that she was happy to hand over her weaponry.

Just then, the dog bounded out of the house across the lawn to join them, disregarding her owner in favour of Gabrielle.

"She senses when something isn't right," he explained, and reached out to ruffle the dog's ears. "Don't you Madge?"

The dog laid her head on Gabi's lap, batted her long brown lashes, and gave a gentle whine.

"There, there," Gabrielle murmured, to soothe herself as much as the dog. "You're all right, now."

She spent a couple of minutes stroking the Labrador's soft fur and, by the time she looked up again, the world was no longer spinning.

"Sorry about that," she said again, with more than a touch of embarrassment. "I don't usually suffer from vertigo, but…ah…"

"Can hardly blame you," he said, enigmatically, and then rose to his feet. "Stay there, and I'll get us some water. Madge? Fetch."

To Gabrielle's astonishment and delight, the dog ambled across the lawn to where Luke had dropped the paper lunch bags, took a couple of sniffs, then gently nipped the first bag between her teeth and trotted back, where she set it down at Gabi's feet. She did it all over again with the second bag, then sat proudly with her chin tipped up, ready to be praised.

Gabrielle was fulsome with it, and rummaged inside Luke's bag for the ham bone, thinking that she understood now why Nell had been so eager for her to have it. Madge was, quite clearly, no ordinary dog.

Luke returned a moment later carrying a jug of water and two glasses, stopping first to retrieve the bottles of ginger beer the dog had been unable to chomp between its teeth, and set them on the table. Eyeing Madge, who was stretched out on the grass happily gnawing away, he poured a couple of glasses of iced water and then took another look at his patient.

"You seem recovered," he pronounced. "Can I get you anything else?"

"No, no," she said, feeling like a nuisance. "I only came to drop off your lunch; I'd better be going—"

"Why not sit for a while?" he said. "Have something to eat."

"Together?"

His eyes twinkled with mischief. "Do you need a chaperone?"

She glared at him, feeling foolish. "No, it's just...I don't want to intrude."

"No intrusion," he said, easily. "I needed to take a break, anyway."

She remembered that she'd been interested to know what Luke did to earn a crust, and scanned the garden area for any clues. Her eye fell upon a large wooden easel set up at the other end of the lawn beside a folding chair which faced the sea. There appeared to be a canvas affixed to it, smeared with paint, and she looked at the man sitting beside her with renewed interest.

"You're a painter?" she asked.

He nodded. "Amongst other things. I dabble with photography...you know, this and that."

This and that seemed to be doing very well, if his home was anything to go by, she couldn't help but think.

"Can I see—or are you one of those artists who doesn't like people to view their work until its finished?"

He unfolded the sandwich in her bag and placed it in front of her.

"Eat that sandwich and I'll let you see my work in progress. How's that for a deal?"

"Sounds like blackmail but, if you insist…"

She took a healthy bite, and watched him grin at her over the sides, which oozed mayonnaise.

"What?" she asked, self-consciously.

He grinned and shook his head.

"Nothing. Just pleasantly surprised, that's all. A lot of women who look like you tend to eat salad or drink those God-awful protein shakes, before doing five hours of Pilates, or whatever the hell."

Gabi swallowed her second mouthful before answering.

"I used to be like that," she said, honestly. "Living in London, I got caught up in a sort of treadmill—metaphorically and otherwise. I used to worry about what I ate, sugar content and all that. But then, I…ah…I ended up losing too much weight, so I'm trying to regain a bit. I still enjoy Pilates, but I do it for strength rather than weight loss."

"Seems like a smart choice," he said, and she was grateful he hadn't done anything so cliché as remarking on her figure. That didn't mean he hadn't taken a surreptitious look, of course, but whatever his conclusions had been, he'd had the good grace to keep them to himself.

"Nell told me you bought the land from her to build this place," she said, changing the subject. "It's very beautiful."

He took a long swig of ginger beer.

"Thanks," he said, and turned to meet her eyes again. "I fell in love with the view, and I decided I'd like to wake up to it every day."

Gabrielle marvelled at anybody having the confidence to just pick up sticks and follow their heart.

"Not so different to the decision you made," he said, as though he'd read her mind. "You saw something you wanted and went for it."

She supposed she had, and felt the old stirring of something like pride in her belly.

"Most of my friends think I've gone stark raving mad," she said, and, for once, the saying was uncomfortably close to home. "Which reminds me, I need to call them, sometime soon."

"You can probably get a signal here," he said. "Why don't you make your calls and then let me know when you're ready to head back down. I'll be over at the easel."

He rose to his feet, and the dog's head lifted at the same time. He scooped up the paper bags and other remnants of their lunch, before offering one final parting thought.

"It isn't mad to seek peace after a storm, Gabrielle."

With that, he turned to stride back across the lawn.

She watched him disappear into the house and wondered what kind of storm he'd found himself embroiled in.

CHAPTER 10

While Luke settled himself at his easel, Gabrielle retrieved her mobile phone and found he was right: there were two whole bars of signal, and she almost whooped with joy.

Until her phone refreshed itself, and dozens of message notifications began filtering through.

How's the new digs? from Frenchie.

Hope the move goes well, from her mother. *Met someone new, can't wait to tell you all about him. Think he's The One.*

She'd heard that before, and decided that it didn't require an urgent response.

Are you still alive out there? again, from Frenchie, this time with a funny picture of herself at her desk at Frenchman Saunders, looking like she was ready to expire from the workload.

Gabi smiled, remembering a time when that desk had been hers.

She scrolled to the next notification.

I need to borrow some money, from her father. *Call me as soon as you can.*

That was no surprise. Her father had sustained a gambling addition for more than twenty years, which had cost him his marriage and many of the relationships he held dear. For a while, he'd followed the Gamblers Anonymous programme and had remained on the straight and narrow, even landing himself a new job, but given the desperate tone to his message, she imagined things had deteriorated since then.

She sighed, and typed a terse response in the negative.

She was done with bailing him out, and, in any event, she needed to watch the pennies these days.

She was in the process of dialling Frenchie's number, when several e-mail notifications pinged through, one of which caught her attention immediately and had been sent only twenty minutes ago.

From: PC Ian Jepson, Metropolitan Police Victim Liaison Unit

To: Gabrielle Adams

Subject: PRIVATE AND CONFIDENTIAL: RE: CASE NUMBER 24867-MET-HOM

Dear Ms Adams,

Further to our last correspondence in the above matter, I am writing to inform you of a recent development in our investigation.

As you will be aware, colleagues in our Digital Forensics Team have been analysing CCTV footage from all known attack sites in what we believe to be three linked offences, and the surrounding areas. However, whilst that process remains ongoing, officers were called to the scene of a further attack last night, in circumstances identical to your own and the two attacks prior. On this occasion, thanks to another citizen's timely intervention, the perpetrator was apprehended, and an arrest was made shortly after eleven o'clock. The suspect remains in custody and, following extensive questioning throughout the morning, I am informed by my Senior Investigating Officer, DCI John Hassan, that a formal charge of murder will be made and, in your case, attempted murder. We are liaising with the Crown Prosecution Service at the moment.

I understand you will have a lot of questions, and I will endeavour to answer them as the prosecution case goes forward. However, I hope this comes as good news to you, and will bring a measure of resolution following your ordeal. I hope you will understand that it may be necessary for us to obtain further statements from you, and it is likely that you will be summoned to appear in court, when the case goes to trial.

I have attached two images of the suspect, whose name is RICHARD SLATER, and would be grateful if you would let me know if you have any recollection of his face, following the events of 18th December. Please be advised that the contents of this e-mail, including *all attachments, names or personal data remain confidential.*

Best wishes,
PC Ian Jepson

Gabrielle read and re-read the e-mail. Then, with a trembling finger, she clicked to open the attachment.

Her breathing grew unsteady as she waited for the images to load, and the dog looked up from its position at her feet, no doubt sensing the tension that now permeated the air.

Finally, a face materialised.

Gabi stared at it for long seconds, expecting to feel *something*. Anger, perhaps? Fear?

Instead, she felt a strange sort of detachment.

The face that stared back at her was of a white man in his late thirties or early forties. His eyes were unfocused, and he bore the look of someone who had lived a difficult life, perhaps under the influence of drugs or alcohol, judging by the mottled quality of his skin and the dip to his mouth and eyes.

She didn't recognise him at all.

There was no sudden 'Eureka' moment, where the light bulb finally turned on and she could recall seeing him lurking in the shadows of South Kensington station in the moments prior to the fall. She hadn't seen him follow her from the National History Museum, or anything of that kind. He was, quite simply, a face on a page.

And yet, that face had robbed her of so much.

Her physical health, for a while. Her mental health and, arguably, every aspect of her life as she'd known it.

"Bastard," she breathed, and set the phone away from her with a clatter.

She stared out across the garden, thinking back over what PC Jepson had said. Did the news of an arrest bring a sense of resolution? Yes and no. In the beginning, she'd imagined one specific person coming after her, to finish the job they'd started. That paranoia had since morphed into something much bigger, until she'd learned to fear almost everyone she met and jump at every unexpected noise. It was a constant struggle to remain rational, day to day, and it was only achieved by reminding herself that people were mostly good.

She'd been unlucky, that was all.

Still, it was a comfort to know that Richard Slater, the so-called 'Tube Killer of London' could hurt no more women like her.

Perhaps, in time, that would help her to sleep at night.

Once she'd gathered her thoughts and pasted on what she hoped was a 'normal' expression, Gabrielle made her way across the lawn to where Luke was seated beneath the shade of a palm tree. He made quite a picture, with the sun burnishing his hair a dark, mahogany brown and the sea breeze swaying the leaves in a gentle rhythm at his back. He held a long, slim paintbrush in his right hand and a palette in his left, while a number of half-squeezed tubes of oil paint were scattered on the ground at his feet.

The Artist at Work.

Her footsteps had been silent across the springy grass, but Madge gave her away, lolloping behind with a wagging tail and a snuffle.

"Be with you in a sec," he said, leaning in to dab a few brush strokes here and there.

She moved around to get a better view of the developing canvas, and loved it, instantly. The image was unfinished, but she could see how it would be: rich, textured swirls of colour depicting the sea at night, with a deep navy-blue sky speckled by moon and stars shining down upon a lone boat, carrying a single passenger to an unknown destination. The style reminded her of Turner, who had long been one of her favourite artists, but there was an edginess to his sleight of hand that differentiated the two and made Luke's work more modern.

"Please, don't let me disturb you," she said, while her eyes roamed the canvas. "I've just come to say, 'goodbye', and to thank you again for the help, earlier."

Luke grabbed a nearby rag, dipped it in some sort of solution and began massaging the end of the paintbrush to clean it, before turning to look at her.

"I'll walk you back down the hill," he said. "Just give me a minute to wash up."

"There's no need—"

He and the dog simply stared at her with matching expressions of patience, which was far more effective than any argument might have been.

"All right," she relented. "Just in case I—"

Fall, she'd been about to say.

"—have another funny turn," she said instead.

"Do you want to come in and freshen up, before you head back?"

She'd only have been lying to herself, if she'd refused a chance to snoop inside his spectacular home, and so she accepted.

CHAPTER 11

Inside, every wall had been painted white against a polished oak floor, which might have looked stark were it not for the bold splashes of colour provided by the many paintings, etchings, charcoal and pen-and-ink drawings, photographs and sketches that hung from it. Every one of them was different, and many bore the signature, 'L. Malone', which told her that he was not a man to be pigeon-holed into one style of artistry.

"It's so eclectic," she said, before she could help herself.

Luke shrugged.

"Little bit of this and that," he said, modestly, and didn't prod her for an opinion, as some might have done. During her time working with authors, she'd found many of them couldn't help but seek reassurance, and it had been part of her job to give it to them—or convey the opposite. On the contrary, Luke Malone was a man who needed no reassurance of his own skill, and, she had to admit, she found his quiet confidence attractive.

"Cloakroom's through there," he said, pointing towards a door off the open-plan living space. "Help yourself to whatever you need."

He kept a tidy ship, she was pleased to see, upon discovering his facilities were sparkling clean—which was more than could be said of herself at that moment.

She almost laughed.

Her hair had grown very long, over the past six months, so she'd tied it up into a ponytail before starting her morning shift at the bookshop. It was now coming loose, so that wisps of hair stuck to the sides of her temples. She wore no make-up and, whilst she'd always had good skin, she found herself wishing she'd thrown on a bit of mascara and some concealer to hide the bags beneath her eyes, which were growing so deep, they'd soon be big enough to carry shopping.

On the topic of 'shopping', she really needed to take a trip into Luddo to pick up some home supplies, and made a mental note to ask Nell for the name of a local taxi firm or for details of the closest bus stop.

Without thinking, she turned on the tap for a second time, and re-washed her hands.

Once…

Twice…

A third time.

Her eyes grew sad in the mirror above the vanity unit, and tears sprang forth as she scrubbed at her skin, hating herself and the illness that drove her to do things in sets of three.

Why three, for goodness' sake? Why not five, or ten?

It was an arbitrary number her psyche had clung to but, as her psychiatrist had told her, she should look for the positives in a situation, rather than catastrophizing the negatives.

Implementing his advice, she told herself it was a good thing she'd chosen the number 'three', and not anything more onerous. The next time, she'd try to be satisfied with 'two'.

For now, she finished a third round of hand-washing, towelled herself off and re-arranged the soap so that it was parallel to the edge of the sink.

There.

Order restored, she headed back out into the living room, where she found Luke had changed from his painting clothes into a fresh pair of shorts and t-shirt.

She wondered if he'd heard the tap running for so long but, if he had, he said nothing about it and gestured towards the door, pausing to pick up his keys and whistle for the dog.

"I'm heading into Luddo, after I've taken Madge for a walk," he said, as they made their way back towards the path. "Do you need anything, while I'm there? Nell mentioned you don't have any wheels, yet."

The man must be telepathic, she thought.

"I—well, I was going to ask if there was a local bus route," she replied. "How far is it to walk into Luddo?"

"It's only a couple of miles," he said. "But the road isn't pedestrian-friendly—there aren't any pavements, for one thing. As for a bus, there's a Saturday service that stops at the car park once in the morning, around eight o'clock, and then does a return trip six hours later, around two in the afternoon, once it's been to all the other little villages in this part of the county."

"That's it?"

He grinned. "Most people drive or cycle. I guess Nell forgot to mention that, too?"

Gabi sighed. "I should have told her I'm not—um—"

"Wait there," he said, suddenly, and turned to jog around the side of the house.

"What's he doing now, Madge?" Gabi wondered aloud, but the dog just gave another one of its smiling 'woofs' and rolled over to be scratched. Since they weren't going anywhere, she obliged, and sat beside her on the soft turf to administer a thorough belly rub.

Presently, there came the metallic whine of cogs turning, and she looked up to see Luke steering an old-fashioned pedal bike across the lawn, painted in a powder blue with baskets at the front and back.

"Thought this might come in useful, for you," he said.

Gabrielle looked at the bike, which was wonderful, then again at the man.

"What do you keep back there? An emporium?" she said, disbelievingly.

"Oh, you know. Dead bodies, bats, manly tools and whatnot. This belonged to—"

He looked awkward, suddenly, and then shrugged it off.

"—well, it's no secret," he muttered. "I was married for three years. This bike belonged to my wife."

That prompted all kinds of questions, none of which Gabrielle felt able to ask.

"It's just sitting in the garage gathering dust, so you're welcome to have it, until you find something better. Of course, I understand if you'd rather not."

Some women might have had reservations, but Gabi had never been one to cut off her nose to spite her face.

"This is so kind of you," she said, reaching out to clasp the handlebars. "It's been a while since I've ridden a bike, so I hope the old saying is true."

"We'll find out," he smiled, and let her wheel it across the lawn until they came to the top of the path, where he took the handlebars once more so that she would not have to push the bike down the hill. "Now, then. Would you rather I walked ahead of you, or go side-by-side? There's a handrail you can hold on to, over there."

She hadn't noticed it before, probably because it was half-covered with trailing leaves, but there was indeed a handrail. She gripped it with her right hand and then risked taking a proper look at the return journey, steeling herself against any nausea that might follow.

But this time, it didn't.

She stood still while her system levelled itself, and then sent him a relieved smile.

"I'll be fine now," she said.

He studied her face, and seemed satisfied with what he saw.

"I never thanked you for bringing my lunch," he said, after they'd walked a few metres in companionable silence, with only the scratching of the dog's paws and the whine of turning wheels to disturb them. "I always come down to the café for lunch at around twelve, but I got caught up in work, today. I guess Nell wondered what had become of me."

So that explained it, Gabi thought.

"She's a caring person," she said.

"Nell's one of the best," he agreed. "She force-fed me every day for a week after Isobel left, and clucked around like a mother hen. I don't know what I would have done without her."

Gabi looked across at his profile, which was unreadable.

"I'm sorry," she said, not knowing what else to say. "It's hard to imagine anyone not loving the home you've built, or—"

She broke off, thinking it was none of her business.

"The house wasn't finished, then," he said quietly. "In fact, we were renting the cottage next to yours, which was still being renovated. A lot has changed in the past two years."

He chose not to say anything more, and Gabrielle didn't pry.

Everyone was entitled to their secrets.

CHAPTER 12

Luke deposited the bike around the back of Gabrielle's cottage, promised to pick up a bag of essentials for her whilst he was in town, and they exchanged farewells—she to return to the bookshop, and he to walk the dog along the headland towards Lizard Point, now that the sun was beginning its slow descent and the air was cooler than before.

"Five more minutes and I was planning to send out a search party," Nell joked, when she stepped back into the kitchen.

"Sorry, I ran a bit over—"

"I'm only joking, love. As I said, you're not on the clock until Monday, and I'm glad you're getting to know Carnance. Got a little bit of sun on your cheeks too, I see."

Gabi smiled, and slipped on a bright red apron emblazoned with the Carnance Books & Gifts logo, which consisted of two sides of a seashell, designed to resemble an open book.

"How'd you like Luke's place?" Nell asked, while she sliced off a large slab of chocolate cake for one of her patrons. "Somethin' else, isn't it?"

"It's beautiful," Gabi replied, and began re-arranging some of the items on the countertop. "I can't imagine a more perfect setting for an artist."

Nell watched her fiddle with the sauces and pots, and wondered if Gabi was aware that she'd begun re-arranging them all over again.

Probably not.

"Lucky he's a good artist, or else I'd have sold him the Surf Shack, instead," she chuckled. "By the way, a delivery of books came, while you were gone."

Gabrielle's face lit up.

"Where—?"

"Don't worry, I haven't opened the boxes yet," Nell said, indulgently. "To book nerds like you and me, that's the best part."

Like a couple of kids on Christmas morning, they took themselves off to the storage room and tore into the large brown packages, umming and ahhing over some of the latest releases, debating covers and styles, and which they might choose as their 'Book of the Month'.

"There's one thing I've never really wanted to get into," Nell said, while they arranged some of the crisp paperbacks on the shelves.

"What's that?" Gabi wondered.

"Book politics."

"Books on politics? There are some fantastic current affairs—"

"No, kiddo, I like reading books *on* politics…I'm talking about the politics *of* books."

Ah, Gabi thought.

"I don't like any of this, 'You scratch my back and I'll scratch yours' nonsense," Nell continued, pausing briefly to hand a brightly-coloured children's book to one of her younger patrons. "If I like a book and want to sell it in my place, that's one thing. If my customers have a demand for a book, that's another. But I'm not putting any book on a shelf just because some bigwig publisher wants to pay me for table space. We make enough money here to get by, and with a bit of careful management from my lovely new manager, Carnance Books can carry on being the place people want to come to and spend their money. D'you know what I mean?"

Gabi knew exactly, and realised she'd found another reason to love her new employer.

"You're saying you want to run the bookshop with integrity, without feeling external pressure to stock any particular book," she said.

"Exactly."

"I don't see any problem with that," Gabi said. "After all, people can always order in a book they particularly want, can't they?"

Nell nodded.

"In point of fact, I've had a few ideas about that expansion you were thinking of," Gabi said, while she flipped the spine of a book, so it was facing the correct way up.

Nell paused, all ears now. "Well, step into my office, and let's hear them," she said, and pointed towards an empty window seat, the café having quietened down after the lunchtime rush.

"The first thing concerns shelving."

"Shelving?" Nell said, in surprise. "What's the matter with my shelves?"

"Nothing," Gabi said. "But people who come into a bookshop like to get the benefit of seeing the full cover. They want to see the artwork, a bit like a gallery, and be able to touch the books, to hold them. It's a sensory experience."

"So what do you suggest?"

"I was thinking of more open bookshelves, a bit like we have in the children's section, where we can set the books facing outwards."

"Won't that cut down on available shelf space?"

Gabrielle considered the shop's layout, and shook her head.

"Not with some re-arranging," she said. "If you wrap the new shelves all around the room, on every wall, and put some tables in the middle portion, you'd get a third more shelf space to make up for any that might be lost with the new approach. I measured it earlier."

Nell sat back, imagining how the shop might look, and decided she liked it.

"What else do you have in mind?"

Gabi smiled, her enthusiasm adding a sparkle to her eyes.

"Well, you've got the terraced area outside for overflow seating, which is great, but what about adding a covered canopy area, or an outside 'Books Stall' which also does takeaway coffees? You know the kind I mean?"

"Like an old Italian-style barista cart, which does books too? I like it," Nell said, turning to look out at the terrace. "It would be weather dependent, but then, people come here during rain or shine."

"That's what I thought," Gabi agreed. "Thinking along the mobile lines, I saw that you're already running an ice cream service down on the beach—"

"One of us takes the ice cream barrow down to the beach a couple of times a day when it's extra hot, so that sunbathers don't have to leave their spot," Nell said. "It makes a decent return."

"No reason why you couldn't include a 'Books Barrow,'" Gabi suggested. "It could be a curated selection of our most popular titles, those most likely to be read on the beach."

"I could do a deal—buy one title, get the next half price, or something like that," Nell thought aloud.

"Depending on how far you want to go, there's always the possibility of building another 'Books 'n' Coffee' stall right next to the Surf Shack, so it doesn't ruin the ambiance of the beach," Gabi said. "The idea isn't to lose the charm of the cove."

Nell nodded, considering the possibilities.

"In time, I was thinking you could set up a mobile bookstore," Gabi continued, on a roll now. "This is the only independent bookshop for miles around, but there are countless villages and towns scattered within a radius of here. In that case, why not take the show on the road, and offer a weekly bookshop-cum-coffee-shop in some of these places?"

"Bring the books to the people, you mean?"

"For those who can't make it to Carnance," Gabi agreed. "You'd need to renovate a van or something, and hire a driver, but aside from that—"

"Anything else, while you're spending my lottery winnings?" Nell enquired.

Gabi grinned.

"As a matter of fact…I wondered why you hadn't thought to add on a conservatory on that side of the shop," she said, pointing to an area of unused space on the cliff side of the building. "It's going to waste at the moment, but we could use a covered area for more tables, or more shelves. Better yet, I could put it to use as an events area, for visiting authors or school trips."

Nell shifted in her seat to visualise the space, annoyed that she hadn't thought to do it before now.

"We turn away more people than we can seat," she said. "There's never any shortage of customers, so there's no reason the costs couldn't be recouped. Besides, I like the idea of providing a space for local schools to use from time to time, or somewhere that could be hired out."

She looked across at her new manager and nodded.

"Put together some costings for me, and we'll talk again."

"I'll make a start tonight."

"Don't forget, you're having dinner at my place this evening," Nell reminded her. "Actually, I meant to ask: you don't have any weird food intolerances that'll give you the runs, do you?"

Gabrielle laughed, thinking of how that question would have been received amongst her gluten-free, lactose-intolerant, vegan-plant-based-diet-eating friends back in London.

"Not that I'm aware of," she said, solemnly.

"Thank God for that."

CHAPTER 13

Dinner at Nell's house was very similar to the woman herself: warm, wholesome, and generously proportioned.

"More potatoes, love? You've hardly eaten a morsel."

Gabrielle looked down at her plate, which was already heaped with food, and waved away the extra carbs.

"I'm holding out for dessert," she said, truthfully. "I heard Pat's sponge cake is a religious experience."

The woman herself smiled proudly from her position across the long dining table.

"Amen to that," Luke chimed in. "It's lucky you're a happily married lady, Pat, or else I'd be giving Jude a run for his money."

"Aye, and you'd have a belly like mine to show for it," her husband quipped, to make them all laugh.

As she sat there basking in the warmth of her neighbour's home and hearth, listening to the easy banter carrying on around her, Gabrielle thought she felt something begin to uncoil, finally, deep in her belly. Whether it was the company, or the news she'd received from the Met Liaison Officer earlier that day, or both, she didn't care; all she knew was that she was feeling more relaxed than she'd felt in a very, very long time.

Gabrielle had refused any alcohol, in deference to the tablets she was taking, but nobody seemed to care, and she happily sipped a glass of sparkling water while she studied the faces of those seated around the dining table beside her. At the head was Nell, of course, who was happily flitting to and from the adjoining kitchen—which was a triumph of interior architecture, and any culinary person's dream. Their hostess had chosen to wear a pretty, multi-coloured dress and sandals with tiny bells and other embellishments on them, which jangled as she pottered about and further reinforced Gabi's notion of her having been some sort of pirate in a previous life.

Jackson was seated at the other end of the table, and his aftershave occasionally coincided with the current of air flowing from a large fan in the corner of the conservatory, travelling the short distance to assail her nostrils with its overpowering scent. She was seated in the middle with Jude beside her, while Luke and Pat were seated opposite. Dotted around the remaining seats were four other people whom Nell had introduced as 'good friends from Luddo', consisting of a couple by the name of Jane and Pete Lander who Gabi judged to be a few years older than herself, and another couple in their sixties who introduced themselves as Barbara "Call me Babs" and Mike Chegwin.

"So, Gabi, tell us about life in London," Jackson said suddenly, and several pairs of eyes turned towards her with polite interest. "Do you miss it?"

She considered the question, and found the answer surprisingly easy.

"No," she said. "I miss some of my friends, but not enough to keep me living somewhere that no longer makes me happy."

"That's how I felt about Birmingham," Pat said. "Once I'd seen this place and met Jude, I couldn't imagine going back to my old life."

"I envy you, living down here at the cove," Jane remarked. "If there was a house big enough for all of us, I'd have snapped it up from Nell long before now!"

"We've recently had our second child," her husband explained, for Gabi's benefit. "It's a madhouse, most days."

"All right for you to say, since you'll be back in the office from September," Jane said, with a playful nudge. "It'll be muggins, here, manning the fort during term times."

"I work over at the university in Falmouth," Pete explained. "I teach Marine Biology."

"That must be fascinating," Gabi said, thinking of deep sea diving and David Attenborough documentaries.

"It beats having to deal with the drunk and disorderly," he said, with a smile for his wife.

"Don't forget the drug offenders and the pickpockets," Jane said, and rolled her eyes.

"Jane here is our local bobby," Jackson said. "Although, I should call you by your official title, Detective Sergeant Jane Lander."

"I'm not on duty," she said, good-naturedly. "In fact, I don't officially return from maternity leave until Monday morning. That leaves one whole day left to enjoy watching daytime telly and walks on the beach with Hattie."

"You're meeting all the emergency contacts you'll ever need, tonight, Gabi," Nell intoned. "Mike here is our local GP, so you'll probably want to register with his practice."

"Mates rates," he said with a wink, in the full knowledge that medical care was provided for free as part of the National Health Service.

Gabi felt her heart rate soar, as a direct response to the sudden stress invading her body. In London, going to see one's doctor was an anonymous affair that nobody needed ever to know about. In Carnance, it seemed the local doctor was firm friends with her employer, and an old-fashioned pillar of the community. Whilst she was sure he would respect doctor-patient confidentiality, the mere thought of her new neighbours...her new *friends* learning of the extent of her neuroses was enough to dampen her mood and make her think twice about the aforementioned sponge cake.

"Hey, speaking of the Big Smoke, did you hear they've found that Tube Killer?" Mike continued, blithely. "One thing I think we can say for certain, Gabi—you won't find anyone like that, down here!"

Immediately, Gabi could feel a panic attack coming on, and set her knife and fork down on her plate, very carefully. She smiled when she was supposed to, mumbled something about needing the bathroom and rose to her feet, intending to find a quiet space in which to battle through the anxiety and regain her composure.

But she was too slow.

The faces around her became a blur, their voices a drone in her ears, and she began to see white spots in front of her eyes moments before she did the very thing she'd sworn never to do again.

She fell, and there was nothing she could do to prevent it.

"Give her some room!"

Nell's imperious order was largely for Jackson and Luke's benefit, both men having been swift off the mark in hurrying around the dining table to reach their damsel in distress and, presumably, administer any kisses of life that might have been required.

"Gabi? Can you hear me?"

Mike knelt beside her, all traces of joviality gone as he reverted to clinical mode.

"Yes," she whispered, and then winced as a sharp pain throbbed at the back of her head.

"Where does it hurt?"

She raised a shaking hand to point out the position on her skull, which had connected with the hard tiled floor.

"There?" he asked, and ran gentle fingers over the area. "Okay. Nell? We're going to need something we can use as a cold compress."

She nodded, and hurried back to the kitchen.

"Now, I'm going to ask you to try and sit up, very slowly," Mike said. "No sudden movements, all right?"

She nodded and, taking his hands, moved into an upright position.

"That's good," he said. "Now, let's move you somewhere more comfortable—let's go for one of the armchairs in the living room."

Further offers of help were given, but Mike was more than capable of escorting her to a chair, which he achieved with the minimum of fuss. Once there, he accepted the cold compress from Nell then dispatched the stragglers to have a moment alone with his new patient.

"Well, Gabrielle, I need to ask you a couple of questions," he said, once she was settled and her colour had come back. "You gave us all a scare, back there. Do you think you might be pregnant?"

She might have laughed, if the thought of how long it had been since she'd had sex wasn't a topic worth crying over. Perhaps she should be asking the medical professional whether there was any chance her body might have closed up shop for good.

"No," she said, deciding that kind of humour was probably misplaced, in present company.

"Do you suffer from dizzy spells very often?" he asked her, obviously working through a checklist in his mind while he measured the pulse at her wrist.

Gabi decided to help him out.

"I don't suffer from low or high blood pressure," she said, keeping her voice down. "I had a panic attack, back there."

His brow furrowed.

"Do you know what triggered it?"

"Yes."

She didn't want to go into it, and he seemed to understand.

"Are you taking any prescribed medication?"

She nodded. "It's in my bag, which I left in the hallway," she said softly. "I was hoping to make it in time to take a beta-blocker, but I was too slow."

"All right," he said, giving her hand a fatherly pat. "I think you should come and visit me on your next day off, and we'll do a proper assessment. If you let me have your details, now, I'll ask our office technician to register you urgently at the surgery, so your records can be transferred from London sooner rather than later. Does that sound all right?"

Gabi nodded. "I planned to come into Luddo and do all of that anyway," she said. "It will save me some time."

He checked her pupils and pulse again, then gave a nod.

"Keep that cold compress on your head for a while, it'll help keep any swelling down," he advised. "I'd rather you stayed on here for another hour or so, for observation, before you head home for the evening."

"Oh, but I'd rather just leave—" she said, feeling every possible degree of embarrassment after what had just happened.

"Gabrielle," the doctor said, gently. "You've no need to feel ashamed because you fainted on Nell's floor. For one thing, Jude passed out cold only last Christmas, after sampling one too many glasses of her special punch. We had a hell of a job getting him back down the hill and safely into bed."

Gabi smiled at that.

"How's the invalid?" Nell enquired, sticking her head around the door.

"She'll live," Mike said, with a wink.

"Well, just in case there's any doubt, I've got some special medicine for you, right here."

She held out a plate laden with an enormous slice of Pat's sponge cake.

"Think you can manage it?"

Gabi nodded.

"I'm sure I can force it down—but, I'll...I'll come back through to the dining room and have it with everyone else."

"That's the spirit," Mike murmured, and they walked back through together to face the crowd of well-wishers.

Once all the expressions of concern had been fielded during the course of dessert, Nell's friends from Luddo were obliged to leave before the tide rolled into the cove, cutting off their exit. Gabrielle joined the other residents of Carnance in bidding them all a fond farewell, and she reiterated her promise to Doctor Chegwin that she would pay him a visit at the surgery very soon.

Once the door had shut behind them, Pat and Jude declared themselves tired and left soon after, with only Luke remaining to help clear away the dishes with the other three.

Gabrielle sensed his eyes on her as they gathered up spent pudding bowls, and turned to face him.

"I can almost hear the thoughts turning around in your head," she said. "Why don't you just spit them out?"

Luke glanced towards the kitchen, where Nell and Jackson were loading the dishwasher, and then back at her.

"All right, then. I was wondering if you were ever planning to tell Nell about what happened to you in London."

Gabrielle stared at him for a long moment, then her eyes fell away.

"I didn't realise you were nosy, as well," she said, tautly.

"Hardly that," he said, with a flicker of irritation. "When Nell told us she'd hired someone from the city, I ran a quick Google search and your name came up in connection with more than just publishing."

"You Googled me?"

"Yeah, and don't sound so shocked. People do it all the time."

She could hardly argue with that, since she planned to search 'Luke Malone, artist' at the first opportunity.

"You've known all along why I came here, then."

"Sure, but it doesn't make any difference to me *why* you came. It only matters who you are while you're here."

She swallowed a sudden constriction in her throat.

"I'm surprised Nell didn't do the same—look me up, I mean."

"Maybe she has," Luke said. "But she hasn't mentioned it to me, which she probably would have done. Look, what happened to you in London doesn't affect your work, so it's up to you. But when you live somewhere close-knit like this, you've got two ways of looking at the world: the first is to think that telling people your troubles constitutes an intrusion of privacy you could do without, and you'll damn well carry on washing your hands however many times, flicking light switches or whatever else, and hope that people won't notice…which they will, by the way. The alternative is to acknowledge that you've been fortunate enough to land somewhere full of people who care why you're a nervous wreck, will make allowances, and try to help you, if they can. It's just food for thought."

Gabi listened to him, at first defensively, but then with a degree of admiration.

He was right, of course, but she wasn't about to tell him that.

"You noticed I wash my hands more than once?"

"Anyone with eyes in their head would notice," he told her.

At that moment, Jackson wandered back in and looked between the pair of them.

"Interrupting something?"

"Not at all," Luke said. "I was just about to ask Gabi if she wanted me to walk her home."

He turned to her with a challenge in his eyes.

"Um, that's kind of you, but Doctor Chegwin suggested I stay here for an hour, to make sure I don't have some kind of concussion," she said. "If Nell and Jackson don't mind, that is."

On the contrary, Jackson perked up considerably.

"We don't mind, at all," he said, smugly. "I'll walk you home, myself, when you're ready."

"It's all settled, then," Luke said, with an incline of his head. "Enjoy the rest of your evening."

With that, he took himself off to find Nell.

CHAPTER 14

Though Gabrielle was loath to admit it, Luke was right: she knew she'd been fortunate to find herself in the company of good people, and that she was not half so clever in concealing her little anxious tics as she'd thought she was. Her display that evening had been a perfect example of how quickly her composure could crumble and, in all good conscience, she could not go on concealing an important part of her personal history which might, at any moment, lead to another very public episode.

What if she had another panic attack whilst she was working at the bookshop, or representing Nell's business in some other capacity?

Aside from all that, she was tired of feeling ashamed of who she was—or, rather, who she'd *become*—and it was time to come clean.

"Are you feeling better, love?" Nell asked, when, shortly after ten o'clock, they sat down in her living room armed with mugs of camomile tea.

"Much better," Gabi replied. "Thank you for letting me trespass a bit longer on your time—I know it's getting late."

"Makes no difference to us," Nell replied, as Jackson came in to join them. "We'd only have been lounging in front of the telly, worrying about whether your head was hurt more badly than we thought."

Gabi touched a hand to the bump beneath her hairline, and grimaced.

"I didn't mean to give everyone such a fright," she said.

"Scared five years off me, you did," Nell joked. "Luckily, I've been sipping from the Fountain of Youth all these years, so I'll be able to stand the loss."

Jackson snorted, and she threw a cushion at him, half-heartedly.

"Did you hear that? No respect for his old mum," Nell complained.

"Did the doc have any ideas what caused you to faint?" Jackson asked, with the kind of open tactlessness that Gabrielle was growing accustomed to.

"I've been worrying you had too much heat, working in the kitchen with me today," Nell said, with a frown of concern. "After all your travel, yesterday, there I was, pushing you to do a full shift—"

"Please don't blame yourself," Gabrielle said quickly. "I know exactly what caused me to faint, and it has nothing to do with the heat or having worked too hard."

They looked at her, expectantly.

Now or never, she thought, and took a fortifying sip of tea.

"You...ah, you remember Mike mentioned about the Tube Killer having been apprehended in London today?"

They nodded, seemingly perplexed by the odd turn in conversation.

"Yes, but—"

"The so-called Tube Killer pushed two women to their deaths back in November and December, last year. He pushed a third woman, and she survived, and a fourth woman, who also survived."

She looked up from where she'd been staring into the depths of her mug, and met their eyes squarely.

"I was the third woman."

"You—what?"

Jackson leaned forward in his chair.

"You were pushed onto the underground tracks?"

Gabrielle nodded, and continued to grip her mug like a lifeline.

"I don't remember a lot of what happened," she continued. "I have flashbacks, nightmares…that sort of thing, and when the topic comes up, I sometimes pass out on the floor."

She gave them both a tight smile.

"Maybe it's a good thing that you don't remember," Nell said softly, and rose to come and sit beside her, on the sofa. "I can't imagine how harrowing that must have been."

She put a warm hand over Gabrielle's and gave it a squeeze.

"I thought that, at first," Gabi said, when she could speak again. "But, you see, it isn't just that I don't remember the moments around when…around when I fell. It's that I don't remember big chunks of my life in the hours, days and sometimes in the month before it."

She dragged in a shaking breath.

"Of course, I remember the important things, like my name, my age, my family and other people I know. I wouldn't really have known there were things I'd selectively forgotten, were it not for the fact my old boss might refer to a conversation we'd supposedly had, and I had no memory of it. Or Mark—"

"Mark?" Jackson asked.

"He was my fiancé," she said, in a toneless voice. "He would mention something I'd supposedly said, or done, and I'd have no memory of it. It was very upsetting, because I'd always been so conscientious, so diligent at work. Nothing ever slipped by me, at all."

"I can't see much too slipping by you now," Nell was quick to say. "I don't doubt what you're telling me, but it isn't as if you're walking around the bookshop like Forgetful Frannie. You haven't missed a single thing from an order, or anything like it."

"I've only done one shift," Gabrielle said, but was grateful for the vote of confidence. "I applied for the job here because, despite all that, it shouldn't affect my work," she said. "I can sell books, I can run a business and deal with all sorts of people—that's one thing that has improved, over the past few months. At first, I was very agoraphobic; I didn't want to leave my home, or meet new people, because I didn't trust them. But that's slowly improved, and I haven't felt worried serving customers or speaking to anybody who comes into the shop."

"I've heard nothing but compliments about how friendly you are," Nell assured her. "We've all taken to you, love."

"Definitely," Jackson drawled, and his mother rolled her eyes.

"The fact is, I didn't mention any of this because I wanted to put it all behind me and start afresh; I genuinely thought I had myself under control. But tonight—"

Gabrielle broke off, and set her mug on a nearby coffee table.

"Nell, I'm still in my probationary period, and I wanted to give you the opportunity to re-think your kind offer. I dread to think I'd have a panic attack like that in front of any of your customers and, the fact is, I can't be sure that I won't. I would never want to be a source of…of embarrassment…"

"Stop right there," Nell said, firmly, in a tone she might have used on an unruly toddler. "In the first place, you were under no obligation to state any of this when you applied for the job but, as it happens, I already knew when I hired you."

"You—you did?"

"Of course," she sniffed. "We might be rural, but we're not hillbillies. I looked you up, checked out your LinkedIn profile page and all that, to make sure you are who you say you are. That brought up a few articles published around the time of your attack, and a bit about your having left Frenchman Saunders."

Nell paused, allowing that to sink in.

"D'you know what I thought, when I read about what happened to you? I thought, God bless that poor girl for pulling herself together and getting back on the damn horse. Life marches on, whether we want it to or not, and it's up to us whether we ride it or allow ourselves to be carried along. I admire anyone who can pick themselves up like that, Gabi. It demonstrates grit and tenacity, which are both qualities I was looking for in my new manager. You think what happened to you is a negative? It's the opposite, love. It's the reason you got the job over so many others."

Gabrielle looked at her with eyes that shone.

"Thank you," she said simply.

"As for having the odd funny turn...well, who doesn't?"

"Some people make it a way of life," Jackson said, and looked at his mother.

"There he goes again," Nell said, with a laugh. "Mind yourself, boy, especially since these things might be hereditary."

He sent Gabrielle a look of mock horror, which made her laugh.

"All the same, I'm glad you felt you could speak to us about it," Nell continued. "From now on, I want you to just tell me if you ever need five minutes alone, and I'll understand. I don't want you thinking you have to try and hide yourself away. We all have our demons, it's just a question of how we keep them at bay."

"You know," Jackson said, thoughtfully. "Surfing or kayaking can be a great way to relieve tension… amongst other things, of course."

"You mean, like paddle boarding?" Gabrielle asked, sweetly.

Nell let out a roar of laughter, but Jackson was not to be deterred.

"You let me know if you ever want to catch a wave or two," he said. "You might surprise yourself."

Gabrielle thought again of how long it had been since she'd ridden anything, let alone a wave, and wondered just how long she would be able to keep turning down the offer Jackson had so generously extended. She had a feeling he would be a good tutor, well-versed in many techniques, and she was a normal, healthy female, after all.

"I'll keep it in mind," she said.

"In the meantime, you can walk Gabi home," Nell commanded her son. "It's getting late, and we've got work tomorrow."

"Yes, ma'am."

The short walk back down the hill to Gabrielle's cottage was punctuated with extensive commentary from Jackson about how romantic the stars looked that night, and how soothing the sound of the waves lapping against the sand could be. He reached for her hand and kissed it as they reached her front door, in a gesture she imagined he'd seen in a film, sometime, and although she wasn't particularly moved by any of it, Gabrielle was flattered by the attention and grateful that a handsome man would take the time to make her feel attractive and wanted.

All the same, when he leaned in for a goodnight kiss, she found herself turning away so his lips grazed the side of her cheek.

Disappointed but by no means deterred, she heard him turn and whistle his way back up the hill after she'd locked and bolted the door behind her.

Tired, but feeling as though several weights had been lifted from her shoulders, Gabrielle dragged herself upstairs and soon after fell into a deep, dreamless sleep.

CHAPTER 15

One week later

"I'm going to kill him!"

Nell's murderous roar came from the direction of the kitchen, and Gabrielle abandoned the e-mail she'd been drafting to find out what all the fuss was about.

"What's the matter?"

Nell was red in the face, a look that had nothing to do with the soaring temperatures outside nor the fact she happened to be in the throes of menopause.

"My bloomin' son is the matter—that's what! Amy was perfectly happy here and signed up to work for the whole summer," she raged. "Then, all of a sudden, she ups and hands in her notice under the pretext that the commute is too far. She only lives in Luddo!"

Gabrielle didn't have to ask what Jackson had to do with things, because she could take an educated guess.

"Commute, indeed!" Nell said, and made a raspberry sound. "I saw all the canoodling around the back of the shop and the so-called 'surf lessons' after hours. It's the same story every summer. Jackson has his pick of a fresh crop of summer staff and promises them the moon, has a bit of fun with them and moves on to the next. They imagine their hearts are broken, and they can't stand to be within a hundred yards of him—it's me who ends up losing out and being short-staffed!"

Gabi offered her a piece of fudge from a fresh batch made by the incomparable Pat.

"I shouldn't...oh, hell, give it here."

Nell stuffed a square in her mouth and waited for the sugar to work its magical, healing powers.

"Look, you've got enough to think about," Gabi said, avoiding making any remark about Jackson's hand in their present predicament. "Why don't you leave it to me to find someone to take Amy's place? I'm sure there are plenty of locals in need of temp work, over the summer."

Nell made a low sound of disagreement.

"I wouldn't be so sure," she said. "Most of the businesses down here make their living for the year during peak times, so they do the hiring well in advance to make the best of the tourist trade. We might have the advantage of being in a beautiful spot, but not everybody wants to travel here and back, every day. You've got to nab the best ones early."

"All the same," Gabi said, injecting a bit of optimism into her tone. "I'll put the word about and see what I can do."

"Thanks love," Nell said, wearily. "I don't know what to do with him, sometimes."

Maybe tell him to find his own place? Gabi thought, but was too kind to speak the words aloud.

"Don't worry about a thing," she reiterated. "Besides, it's not all bad news. Jackson's doing a really good job renovating that old Italian coffee cart, and Luke has already agreed to paint it for us. With any luck, we'll be able to get it up and running by the end of the month."

Nell brightened at the thought.

"You've moved mountains," she said, happily. "And, as it happens, I had some quotes come back from the builders about that extension we were talking about."

"And? What's the damage?"

"Not as bad as I feared," Nell said. "Of course, I'll be having a word with Keith Par to ask what I've ever done to deserve him trying to rob me of my eyeballs and come back for the sockets, but, once we've come to a right understanding, I expect work will begin as soon as I've signed on the dotted line."

"The construction work shouldn't get in the way of the patrons," Gabrielle thought aloud. "It's mostly around the cliff side of the shop, which nobody uses. There might be the odd bit of noise, but nothing we can't manage. It's a glorified conservatory, after all."

Nell nodded.

"Keith says they could have it done for us by the end of summer," she said. "It's a shame we won't catch the peak season, but we'll still get plenty of footfall come autumn."

"It'll be heated," Gabrielle reminded her. "That makes a big difference. It means we can run events without needing to worry too much about whether it's cold or rainy, outside, so long as people are willing to get here."

"Have you had any more thoughts about which events you might want to run?"

"A few," Gabi said. "I'm putting together a long list of suggested authors, so you can let me know what you think. I was wondering whether it might be a nice idea to throw a bit of a bookish party, to sort of 're-launch' the bookshop, with all the re-vamped interiors and added space?"

"I love a party," Nell said. "Just name the date, and we can start planning."

"Let's wait and see how quickly they can get our event space ready but, all being well, how about the last week of August?"

"Perfect," Nell agreed, and was about to return to serving customers when she remembered something else. "Oh! Before I forget—Luke asked me to pass on a message. We're all invited to dinner at his place on Thursday night."

"All right, thanks."

As Gabrielle made her way back to her desk, she realised she hadn't seen much of Luke over the past week. Then again, they'd both been very busy—she, getting to grips with her new role, and he, with his art. She noticed that he still came down to the café for lunch, most days, and chatted easily with the servers, but hadn't bothered to seek her out and say 'hello'.

So? her mind whispered. *Why do you care?*

"I don't," she muttered to herself, before clamping her lips shut again. It wasn't as if she needed to add 'talking to herself' to an already long list of weird behaviours.

"What's that?" Nell called out.

"Nothing!"

Settling on her desk chair, Gabi shoved all thoughts of good-looking, artistic types from her mind and reached for the stack of mail that had arrived yesterday and which she hadn't yet had time to open.

Bills, she noted. *Invitations, letters from happy customers...*

Then, there were the proof copies of books yet to be published.

When she'd worked for Frenchman Saunders, proof copies had been ten-a-penny to her. After all, she'd seen the original manuscripts and had followed their evolution all the way to being bound in print, so the final book was never really a big surprise. But, nowadays, she wasn't working behind the veil and so it gave her a little thrill to receive a book bound in brown paper and string that was not yet available to the general public.

The first one she opened was a children's book featuring colourful illustrations of dragons on its cover and, reading the first couple of pages, she added it to a 'YES' pile, knowing instantly it would be enjoyed by many of the children who came through their doors. Once she'd finished going through the mail, she'd read the rest of the book and, all being well, contact the publisher and ask if the author would like to come and do a signing and read some of her story to the children at Carnance.

The next one she opened was a forthcoming release by a local chef, which looked similar to many of the other cookbooks they stocked but for which, she knew, there would be a strong local demand. She added that to the 'YES' pile, too, but made a note to order a limited number, only.

Next, she opened a package from her old publishing house containing Saffron Wallows' next literary feat, entitled, *Girl, Not a Woman*. Without needing to read the first page, she knew it would be a hit. The cover was superb, hitting just the right balance between eye-catching colour and classy layout, which reflected the content to be found within. She'd already heard a lot of buzz around this book and knew that the PR machine would be doing its magic, securing radio and television interviews, broadsheet features and all manner of appearances for an author who was, for many people, literary royalty. Gabi had always taken pleasure in publishing Saffron's work while she'd been at Frenchman Saunders and, of all the clients she'd worked with, she was one she missed more than most.

While she couldn't remember her last meeting with Saffron—another side-effect of the amnesia—she knew that Frenchie had taken over much of her old workload and had acquired Saffron's next two novels, and a thought popped into her head.

Perhaps Saffron might like to appear at Carnance Books?

Admittedly, they were small fry in comparison with some of the much larger venues she would likely be visiting on her summer and autumn book tour, but perhaps she would consider it, for old times' sake? They'd always been on very good terms and, although Mark still represented her as an agent, their break-up should have no bearing on her professional engagements.

She added Saffron's book to the top of the 'YES' pile, and decided to read it that very night.

Before then, she needed to find a new member of staff.

CHAPTER 16

The rest of the week passed quickly, with a steady stream of customers passing through the doors of Carnance Books, many of whom were complimentary about the small but meaningful changes that had already taken place under Gabrielle's management. She and Nell had fallen into a very easy pattern, whereby Nell happily left her to manage the bookshop whilst she took care of the café and gifts side of things. Gabi found that she enjoyed the balance between office and front-of-house work, the former giving her a measure of quiet time whilst the latter afforded her the opportunity to grow her confidence dealing with the general public and get to know some of their regulars.

By the time Thursday rolled around, she was glad she'd opted for it to be one of her days off, and woke up with a spring in her step, ready to make the most of it. After a leisurely breakfast on the beach watching the day come alive, she pushed her new bike up the hill to the car park and then joined the country road that followed the line of the cliffs until it reached the nearby village of Luddo, enjoying the burn in her thighs and the wind in her face as she pedalled as fast as she could.

Luddo was a picturesque place, its cottages built almost entirely of Cornish limestone, and with an ancient church in the middle of it all, covered with Virginia creeper. Its small high street was strung with bunting after hosting a recent fête—at which Carnance Books had occupied one of the stalls—and although the streets were not exactly bustling, the place was far from being one of the ghostly, abandoned places left to ruin when its houses were not occupied by tourists. There was a tiny primary school on the outskirts of the village; Dr Chegwin's surgery; a tiny police station manned by Jane Lander and one other officer; an adventure playground, and several small shops selling all manner of homewares, gifts, home-made chocolates and toiletries, as well as a butcher's shop, a bakery and a fishmonger, all of whom she intended to visit before the day was out.

Before then, she made directly for her favourite place of all…

Pat's Patisserie.

Although the lady herself preferred to live quietly in Carnance Cove, Nell was never one to miss a business opportunity, and the two women had decided to open a dedicated sensory haven where sugar-lovers could unite over Pat's frosted creations in the village, as well as being able to enjoy them at Carnance Books & Gifts. For Gabrielle, it offered a taste of the coffee culture she'd enjoyed back in London; one of the things she'd loved was being able to take a manuscript and sit down with a coffee at a bistro table overlooking a garden square. Pat's Patisserie offered the nearest thing within pedalling distance, and she settled herself at one of the pretty outdoor tables to look out across the village green with a flat white and a warm croissant. Her book of choice was *Girl, Not a Woman*, the latest Wallows' novel she'd been working her way through a few chapters at a time, before bed.

Now, as she was nearing the end of what had been a piquant, harrowing yet beautifully-written novel caught somewhere between Nabokov's *Lolita* and Atwood's *The Handmaid's Tale,* she couldn't understand why it felt so...

So...

Familiar.

The feeling remained as she flew through the final chapters of the proof copy, and lingered even after she'd closed the book, which had ended with the line, "...and this, Dear Reader, is my testimony. I was a girl, not yet a woman, and now I live forevermore in the ether between the two, never to be welcomed by either."

Gabi read the line again, and wondered where she'd heard it before. Had she read the manuscript before its publication?

That must be the answer.

She pulled out her mobile phone and, with the luxury of a signal, dialled Frenchie's number in London.

Her friend answered on the second ring.

"Hey, doll! How's it going?"

"Really well," Gabi replied. "How's things with you?"

"Better than ever," Frenchie replied. "I mean, obviously, I'm ready for a holiday...but, can't complain, really!"

"Who's the latest squeeze?" Gabi teased, knowing her friend never stayed with any man for more than two or three weeks at a time.

There was a slight pause, followed by a nervous laugh.

"Oh, nobody you know," Frenchie said. "How about you? Any hotties at the cove?"

The image of a man sitting at his easel sprang to mind, but Gabi chose not to mention it.

"A couple," she replied. "But listen, I wanted to ask you something."

"Anything. Shoot."

"It's about Saffron's latest novel—*Girl, Not Yet a Woman.*"

"It's not out, yet," Frenchie said. "I can send you a proof, if you'd like?"

"Actually, one of your assistants already sent one to the bookshop," Gabi told her.

"Very efficient, I approve. Have you had a chance to read it?"

"I just finished it," Gabi said. "It was excellent, as always."

"You say it like there's a catch."

"It's not that…it's just, you know with the selective amnesia, I'm liable to forget certain things?"

"Yes…I know."

"Well, I wondered if I might have already had sight of Saffron's manuscript, while I was still at Frenchman's? When I was reading it, the content seemed familiar, and I had this overpowering sensation of déjà-vu."

"Hmm," Frenchie said. "It's possible, but I'd say it was unlikely. The manuscript only came to us a couple of weeks after you left. Saffron had been sitting on it for a while, according to Mark."

At the other end of the line, Frenchie could have bitten her own tongue off.

"I mean…her agent only…"

"It's all right," Gabi said quietly. "You can speak his name, you know. It isn't a dirty word."

"I know…I just don't want to hurt you any more than you've already been hurt."

Gabrielle was touched by her friend's concern. Frenchie was, more often than not, like a social butterfly, so it was easy to forget that there was substance beneath the style.

"Honestly, I hardly think of him," she said, and it was true. In fact, she struggled to recall his face with any degree of accuracy.

All the same, she asked the question.

"How is he? Have you seen much of him?"

"What—what do you mean?"

"On the circuit, I mean? I guess you'd have had to deal with him over Saffron's new book, for one thing."

"Oh, yes, of course," Frenchie said, and gave one of her tinkling laughs. "He's the same as ever. Look, I'd love to stay and chat but I've got a meeting soon. Call you later, okay?"

Later could mean any time between then and a week hence, Gabi knew, but she was fine with that. "Sure—have a good one!"

It was only after she'd ended the call that Gabrielle realised she'd forgotten to ask whether Saffron might be persuaded to visit Carnance Books as part of her promotional book tour, towards the end of the summer.

"Damn," she muttered.

Ah well, there was still time. As for having read Saffron's manuscript before, it was obvious she'd imagined that, especially as it hadn't crossed her desk prior to her leaving Frenchman Saunders. She supposed there was always the possibility that Mark had allowed her to have early sight of it, off the books, while they'd still been living together, but the only way to find that out would have been to ring him and ask…which was something she had absolutely no intention of doing.

Setting it aside, she polished off the last of her croissant, chugged back the remainder of her coffee and went about the rest of her day.

CHAPTER 17

For reasons that had absolutely nothing whatsoever to do with wanting to impress Luke Malone, nor inveigle him in any way, Gabrielle took special care with her appearance that evening. For a long time, she'd barely seen her own reflection in the mirror—only a pale imitation of the woman she'd once been. She'd hated seeing the physical embodiment of her reduced mental state; hated to see the tiny grey hairs that had appeared overnight, or the pinched look to her face.

But now, she found she could stand to look at herself again, without self-loathing, and it was liberating.

So, what, if she had a couple of grey hairs? She could dye them if she wanted to…and she *had* wanted to, at one of the hairdressers in the larger town of Penzance, a few miles yonder, on her last day off. As for looking pinched…a healthy, outdoorsy lifestyle and plenty of good food had made an enormous difference to her wellbeing. She'd lost the harrowed, drawn-out expression she'd worn so well, and had replaced it with fuller cheeks and a light tan, so that she resembled the woman she used to be, not the stranger she had become.

Now, as she considered the selection of items in her wardrobe, she found herself reaching for an electric blue dress which had once been a favourite. Though she was nervous to see whether it would feel alien against her skin, she slipped it on and considered herself in the mirror on the back of her bedroom door.

Actually…not bad.

Not bad, at all!

Perhaps the material was still a little loose around the waist, but that didn't matter. In fact, it would allow more room to enjoy dinner, without feeling constricted.

She blow-dried her hair into shiny waves, took the trouble to apply a bit of make-up and then, at the end of it all, wondered if she'd overcooked herself.

Wasn't that typical? she thought, angrily. Was she so conditioned to be scathing and self-critical that she couldn't look at herself, for once, and say, "You know what, kiddo? You look great."

But then, until she'd come to the cove, it had been a very long time since anyone had paid her anything remotely like a compliment. All she'd ever heard from Mark was quibbles and complaints; little digs about her appearance or supposedly well-meaning suggestions about what she ought to do if she wanted to 'make the most of herself'. After a while, it had become all too easy to forget that, before meeting him, she'd never been short of company and, in fact, that had been one of the things he'd found most attractive about her.

Which was sad, really.

Determined not to dwell on the past, Gabi spritzed a bit of perfume on her neck and wrists, re-capped the bottle, then un-capped it again to add a final spritz to her décolleté before heading downstairs.

Nell met her on the pathway outside her cottage and gave her a long whistle.

"Well, don't you look lovely!" she exclaimed. "Do my eyes deceive me, or have you pushed the boat out a bit, this evening?"

"I don't know what you mean," Gabi said, primly.

"Uh huh. Bet you shaved your legs, and other things, too."

"*Nell!*"

"She doesn't deny it," Nell said, wickedly.

Gabi was relieved Jackson wasn't around to overhear their tête-à-tête, otherwise she could only imagine his input to the conversation.

"No Jack, tonight?"

"Nope, he sends his apologies, but apparently he's got—quote, unquote—a *business meeting* to attend in Luddo."

"What kind of business would be meeting at this hour on a Thursday night?"

"The kind with long hair and short shorts," Nell said. "I swear, I don't know where that boy gets his energy."

Gabrielle thought it best not to speculate.

"Thought you might like to know, I've set a start date with the building company," Nell said, as they made their way up the path towards Luke's place. "They'll be on site in two weeks' time, and they say it shouldn't take more than four weeks to have the conservatory completed. Obviously, I'd add on another two weeks to that estimate, which brings us to the end of summer, just as we'd hoped."

"Perfect," Gabi said, excitedly. "Oh, it's going to be great."

Nell smiled. "You're happy here, aren't you, love?"

Gabi stopped and turned back, raising a hand to shield her eyes from the glare of the setting sun as she took in the view of the cove with its little white houses and crystal blue waters, then thought of the kindness all its residents had shown her.

"Yes, I really think I'm happy, Nell."

But even as she said the words, a small voice warned her not to grow too comfortable, for things could change in an instant, as she knew only too well.

When they reached the top of the hill, they found Pat and Jude had beaten them to it and were already happily settled on Luke's terrace with drinks in hand, laughing over something that had been said. With the scent of wild garlic and mint carrying on the warm, early evening air, they might easily have been at a Tuscan olive grove or on some Greek island, and not on the southern shore of England, Gabi thought.

"We come bearing gifts!" Nell called across to them, and waved a bag containing rosemary focaccia and various other antipasti.

For her part, Gabi had brought a bottle of red and a bottle of white wine, both of which she knew to be good.

"Welcome," Luke said, crossing the lawn on long legs which were encased in a pair of well-fitting jeans, Gabrielle happened to notice.

He leaned in to give Nell a kiss on both cheeks, with the kind of easy affection that had been so lacking in the stilted air kisses Gabi remembered from her publishing days. Then, after a second's hesitation, he leaned in to offer the same welcome to her, and she felt the brush of his light stubble against her cheeks and the warmth of his body as it touched her own, albeit briefly.

"A bit chilly tonight, isn't it?" she declared afterwards, crossing both arms over her chest.

"Is it?" he said, while humour danced in his eyes. "Seems rather warm, to me."

Nell watched their by-play with a knowing eye.

"How's that painting coming along?" she asked, to give Gabrielle a moment's respite.

"Getting there," he said. "The sky isn't quite right, but I think I know how to fix it. Another day, and it should be done."

"Is it a commission?" Gabi asked, as they made their way across the grass to greet the others.

"No, this one's for my own pleasure," he said. "It's part of a series of paintings depicting the cove which I plan to show at my gallery in St Ives."

"*Your* gallery?"

"Yes, I have a couple dotted around the place," he said. "There's another in Charlestown, one in Padstow and another in Truro. I try to feature new artists as well as those who are more established."

"That's wonderful," she said, and made a mental note to visit one day.

"You forgot to mention the gallery in London," Nell said, with pursed lips. "He's being modest, Gabi. Luke has galleries around the world, not just here in Cornwall."

A flicker of mild irritation crossed his face, but was quickly concealed.

"Some were inherited," he said, shortly, and let the matter drop. "What can I offer you to drink? Shall we open some of this nice red, and have it with the antipasti?"

There were murmurs of agreement, and the five of them settled down to eat.

They talked and ate while the sun went down, then moved indoors to enjoy coffee and a selection of Pat's pastries on the enormous U-shaped sofa Luke had positioned in front of wide windows looking out to sea. He pressed a button and soft music began to play from speakers dotted around the room, and then wandered around turning on the table lamps, so they could enjoy a soft ambiance to round off the end of a wonderful evening.

"You're a very good host," Gabi said, when he came to sit on the sofa beside her.

"I am when I choose to be," he said, with the flash of a smile. "In the interests of full disclosure, I've also been called a 'miserable, misanthropic git.'"

Gabrielle laughed.

"You look very well," he said, and let his eyes roam over her face. "Life by the sea suits you."

It was the first time he'd shown any obvious regard, and Gabi found herself at a loss. It was hardly the first time she'd been complimented by a member of the opposite sex—and not even the most effusive of compliments, come to that—but he might as well have told her she was the goddess Aphrodite, for all the effect it had on her nervous system.

"Thanks," she said, in that annoying, breathless tone she'd heard other women use and had sworn never to use herself. "I'm starting to feel very much at home in Carnance."

He looked down at his glass, then up again.

"I wondered whether you might like to take a ride out, on your next day off? I could show you some of the other coves…anywhere you'd like to go."

She let out the long breath that had lodged itself in her chest.

"That would be lovely. I've got a day off on Sunday…"

"Perfect," he said. "It's a date."

They smiled at one another and, from their position at the other end of the long sofa, Nell and Pat almost rubbed their hands together with glee.

"What are you two plottin'?" Jude demanded, from behind a copy of one of the magazines he'd picked up from the coffee table.

"Shh! For heaven's sake," Pat told him. "Keep your voice down, you big lummock!"

He eyed them over the rim.

"Best not be match-makin', again. You know it doesn't do, to meddle in affairs of the heart."

"We wouldn't dream of any such thing," Nell said, in a stage whisper. "But, if two people happen to like one another and both have been hurt in the past, well…where's the harm in givin' them a little nudge?"

Jude muttered something beneath his breath.

"Besides," Pat sniffed. "If I hadn't taken it upon myself to meddle with *you*, Jude Barker, then where would you be? You'd be half the man you are, today."

"I won't argue with you, there," he said. "I'd be a damn sight thinner, for one thing."

CHAPTER 18

The little voice inside Gabrielle's head had been right, of course.

The following day dawned brightly enough and, with her thoughts still happily occupied by the prospect of getting better acquainted with a handsome, interesting, creative man who liked books and art, Gabrielle breezed through the working day, scarcely batting an eyelid when plates were smashed, or books were bent out of shape and unable to be sold.

"You've been walking on air, today," Nell said, as they began their clean-up operation at the end of the day. "I take it you enjoyed dinner with a certain tall, dark-haired gentleman?"

"I wouldn't say Jude was tall," Gabi said, and caught the tea towel Nell threw at her with a laugh. "If you're referring to a certain *other* gentleman, then…yes, I had a lovely evening. We all did."

She slung the tea towel over her shoulder and watched as, suddenly, the bathers on the beach began to pack their things away, as if a bell had been rung to signal last orders.

"In fact, he asked me on a…a sort of date. He's going to take me out for the day, on Sunday."

Nell did a little happy dance, jiggling her hips.

"Ooh, now, this is exciting…"

Gabrielle held up her hands.

"Let's not get ahead of ourselves," she said. "I recently got out of a long-term relationship, and so did he."

Nell frowned. "Are you talking about Isobel—his wife?"

Gabi nodded. "Luke told me he was married for three years before Isobel left," she said. "He didn't really go into it any further."

Nell warred between breaking a confidence, of sorts, and making sure Gabi was well informed, especially after the heartache she'd already suffered.

"Isobel *did* leave," she said slowly, lifting a hand to wave off Elena and Zack, the newest member of their serving team whom Gabi had hired only a couple of days before. "But not in the way you might think. Luke's wife died in a boating accident, Gabi. She got caught up in the rip tide over on the western headland, at Gull's Point," she said, referring to a jagged outcrop jutting from the far headland, on the opposite side of the cliffs to the car park.

Gabrielle was aghast.

"When—when did this happen?"

"Almost two years ago," Nell told her. "I'd have thought Luke would have told you himself, but, there again, maybe he was waiting for the right moment."

Or maybe he's still grieving, Gabi thought. *Maybe he loved his wife too much to talk about her death.*

Which put a different complexion on things, she was forced to admit.

"There's a terrible undercurrent at Gull's Point," Nell went on. "You should be careful, if you're ever swimming around that way."

"Jackson already warned me," Gabi said, distractedly. "He pointed out the safe places to swim and paddle-board, and the places I should avoid, as a beginner."

"Good," Nell said. "It's been a long time since we've had any accidents like that, and I hope we never see anything like it again."

"He must have been heartbroken, when they brought her in," Gabi murmured, looking through the long windows of the empty shop and out across the water, to where she imagined the woman had drowned.

When she turned back, Nell had a pained expression on her face.

"That's the worst of it, love. It wasn't Jackson or the coastguard who brought Isobel to shore. It was Luke. He went in after her, but was too late to save her."

Something clutched inside Gabrielle's heart as she imagined Luke kicking out against the current, battling to save his wife, only to collapse on the sand with her lifeless body beside him.

"Has there been anyone else, since her death?"

Nell nodded.

"There've been a couple, but nothing permanent, and nothing *important*, if that's what you mean."

Gabrielle wondered which category she might fall into, and realised she would have to decide whether it was worth finding out.

Gabrielle offered to close up the shop, only too happy to be left alone with her thoughts and the comforting smell of books and baked goods, while Nell headed home for a well-earned break.

As she moved around the shelves re-arranging titles into alphabetical order, turning signs the correct way up and wiping away the dust which seemed to accumulate at the end of every day, she watched the last of the tourists make their way back towards the car park, disappearing around the headland in a slow sort of exodus before the tide closed in. The sky, which had been a bold, cornflower blue for much of the day, was beginning to darken out at sea, with clusters of clouds forming where there had been none before.

Thinking nothing of it, Gabrielle continued rubbing down tables and hoovering crumbs from the floor until, the next time she looked up and out of the long windows at the far end of the shop, the clouds seemed to have tripled in size and were now looking considerably darker.

"Best get a move on," she muttered to herself.

Sea frets were normal in that part of the world, and could come on very quickly, or so it seemed to one who was not well-versed in the fine art of reading the coastal weather. She was sure that, if any of the others had been there, they'd have been able to predict the onset of rain long before the first cloud began to form, but, as a novice in these matters, she was left scrambling to finish her tasks as quickly as she could so that she could dash home without being caught in a downpour.

Sure enough, five minutes later, she heard the first patter of rain on the roof—gentle, at first, but soon growing more insistent as angry storm clouds swept into the cove with alarming speed. As the wind picked up speed, so too did the waves, which crashed against the low harbour wall, their foamy swell thrusting against the limestone rocks with relentless force.

Gabrielle watched it all from the window, at once transfixed and terrified by the power of Mother Nature, which had transformed a quiet, sandy bay into something terrifying and awesome. She found herself wondering if Luke's wife had found herself caught in the eye of a storm like the one which now battered against the little shop; tiny and insignificant against the might of gallons of water whipped into a frenzy.

She shivered as she stood there in the window, arms hugging her body and eyes wide while she watched streaks of lightning tear through the sky, briefly illuminating the gloom of rain and wind, like an eye blinking open and then shut again. She told herself it was time to go home, to lock the shop's door and run the short distance to the little cottage she'd come to call home, and batten down the hatches until the storm passed.

Lightning flashed again.

Then, she saw them.

Nothing more than specks against the sky, two figures stood precariously on the edge of the far headland, above Gull's Point.

She moved closer to the window, peering through it to try to see through the curtain of rain, wondering if they'd been nothing more than a mirage.

Lightning came again, closer than before.

That's when Gabrielle saw it.

She saw one of the figures on the headland take a sudden step forward, with arms outstretched. She saw them push the other with enough force to send them tumbling over the edge of the cliff, their body hurtling through the air, arms and legs kicking out in desperation until the sea claimed them.

Gabi made a strangled sound in her throat, her body shaking in reaction to what she'd seen, and she found she couldn't breathe, as if it were *she* whose body had been swallowed by the water.

"Oh—oh, God—"

She was hyperventilating, but she knew what she needed to do.

She needed to act.

CHAPTER 19

Fighting the rising nausea, Gabrielle stumbled back to the office to reach for the desk phone, intending to call the police, the coastguard—or *someone*.

But there was no dial tone.

Sobbing now, she tried her mobile phone, but found the same story—no signal.

Think, she told herself. *Try to think.*

If the landline was down, possibly because of the weather, that left only the SOS phone on the beach— but it was too near the harbour, and she risked being swept away—or Luke's place, since there was no way of getting to the car park, now. Others lived closer, but none of them would be able to alert the authorities, so it made sense for her to try him first.

She didn't hesitate but ran out into the rain and pelted up the hill, not caring that her clothing immediately became sodden, or that her mascara ran in tiny rivulets down her face. All she cared about was helping that poor woman...

For, it had been a woman who'd fallen, she was sure of it. She'd seen her long, dark hair streaming behind her as she'd fallen over the cliffside, and her body had been small and slight, a lot like...

...a lot like her own.

Gabi felt her stomach roll, and she gritted her teeth, forcing her legs to move faster while she propelled herself up the winding pathway to Luke's house, skidding only once as she neared the summit so that she fell forward, both knees landing in the rough dirt track.

Dragging herself up again, she ignored the pain and let out a small cry of relief as she neared the little white picket gate that gave access to his garden. Rain streamed into her eyes, and thunder crackled overhead as she shoved it open and squelched across the grass, making directly for the house.

Once she reached the double doors that led from the veranda, she grasped the handle and tried to open one of them but found it locked. A moment later, Madge's furry face appeared at the glazed panel, letting out a questioning bark to see who'd come to call.

Gabrielle knocked on the door, and kept knocking as the rain began to permeate her bones and her teeth began to chatter. She peered through the door and called out to Luke, but the house was in darkness beyond.

She didn't see him approach from the garden behind, until he was almost upon her.

"Gabi?"

She let out a scream and spun around, slamming herself back against the door, where the dog let out another confused bark from the other side.

"Hey! Hey, it's only me," Luke said, holding up his hands.

He was dressed for the weather in the same sturdy boots and all-weather coat he'd worn to collect her from the station, the hood pulled up so that his face was in shadow.

"L—Luke?" she stammered, as her body continued to shake.

"Here, let me get the door open, and we'll go inside and warm up," he said, taking in her dishevelled state.

He mounted the stairs and she slid to the side to allow him to unlock the door.

"Come in," he said, holding out a hand to her.

She didn't grasp it, but followed him inside, all her thoughts now centred on calling the police so that the woman's killer could at least be apprehended.

For, as certain as she was that the person who'd been pushed over the cliffside was female, she was equally certain that they would not have survived such a fall in those conditions.

It was murder.

Inside, he gently ushered the dog aside so that he could close the door behind them, blocking out the howling wind and rain, which swept across the lawn.

"You must be freezing," he muttered, as he shouldered out of his raincoat.

Gabrielle couldn't deny it, since her whole body was now shivering badly, and she'd lost the feeling in her extremities.

"I'll get you a towel," he said, and walked quickly to the nearest bathroom.

"Wait—I—I need to find a signal," she said.

"Okay," he replied, from across the room. "Go ahead."

Automatically, she reached for her mobile phone, but realised with a sinking heart that she'd forgotten to pick it up from her desk back at the shop.

"I need to borrow your phone," she called out again.

Luke returned with a towel in hand, which he gave to her. But, instead of using it, she simply held it while her eyes appealed to him, in anguish.

"Please, Luke!"

"All right," he said, growing increasingly concerned. "It's no problem to borrow my phone, Gabi, but I need to ask—are you okay? Your knee is bleeding…"

She glanced down at her bare legs beneath the summer dress she wore—and which was now a semi-transparent sheath against her saturated skin.

"It's nothing," she said, growing agitated again. "The phone?"

He nodded, and reached inside his pocket to pull out his mobile.

"There's a couple of bars," he said. "Here."

He handed it to her, but her hands were so numbed by the cold, she was clumsy and lost her grip.

"Let me help," he said, retrieving it from the floor. "Who do you need to call? Tell me the number, and I'll enter it for you."

"The police," she said. "Call 999."

He looked up again in surprise.

"Police? Gabi, what's happened? Is it to do with the case against Richard Slater—?"

She shook her head.

"I—I can't explain now—I'll tell them everything over the phone."

"Okay, but if you want the police, you'd be quicker calling Jane Lander, direct. She's only in Luddo, so she'd be able to get here much faster than any other car they might dispatch," he said.

Gabrielle saw the sense in that, and nodded.

"All right, could you call her, please?"

Luke nodded, and dialled the number for the local police station, before handing the phone back to her so she could press it against her ear. Then, he took the towel from her limp hands and draped it around her shoulders while she went through the motions of detailing what she needed from the PC who took the call.

How can we help you, today?

"I need to report a murder," Gabrielle said, clearly and succinctly, and Luke's hands stilled against her shoulders.

He listened while she gave a garbled account of what she'd seen, moving around the living room to turn on some of the lights, until she ended the call and handed the telephone back to him.

"Jane's going to go and take a look at the headland, and she says she'll alert the coastguard and let me know if…if anything turns up. She asked where I'd be, in case she needed to call…I told her I'd be here. I hope that's okay."

Luke nodded.

"Of course. It might be worth drying off a bit, before you catch your death."

It was an unfortunate turn of phrase, and he pulled a face, moving towards the open-plan kitchen to set the kettle to boil.

"I thought we could both use a cup of tea," he said. "I heard what you told the constable, Gabi. Do you want to talk about it?"

She shuffled towards the long kitchen island, wincing slightly as the pain in her knee began to penetrate, and slid onto one of the stools.

"I saw a woman pushed off the cliff, over at Gull's Point."

He stopped what he was doing, and turned to face her again.

"At Gull's Point?"

"Yes—and I—I know what happened to your wife," she said. "I'm so sorry for your loss, Luke, but this is different. I saw two people, through the rain…"

"Where were you?"

"Inside the shop," she said, accepting the steaming cup he offered her. "I was closing up for the day, when the storm came in. I saw what happened, through the window."

"And what did you see?"

She paused to take a sip of tea, letting the scalding liquid warm her from the inside out.

"Lightning lit up the sky and sort of…cut through the rain. When it did, I saw two people standing on top of the headland, very close to the edge. That made me nervous to begin with, because I couldn't understand why anybody would be standing out there with the storm raging all around. Then, all of a sudden, one of them just…they just…"

She sucked in a long, quivering breath and closed her eyes.

"They put both arms out and shoved her off the edge, into the sea."

Luke leaned forward, resting both forearms on the countertop.

"How do you know it was a 'her'?"

Gabrielle opened her mouth, then closed it again.

"I—well, I suppose I can't be one hundred per cent sure of anything, but every instinct told me it was a woman. One with long, dark hair...wearing a bright blue jacket, I think," she added, having remembered the flash of colour as she fell.

Luke said nothing for a moment, and she became defensive.

"I know how it sounds," she said, the shock and the horror of what she'd seen beginning to set in. "*Paranoid Gabi, imagining things, again.*"

"Nobody has accused you of that," he said quietly.

"But they will," she said, miserably. "I know what people will think—that I've hallucinated the whole thing. It's happened once or twice before."

"It doesn't matter what might have happened in the past," he said. "Do you believe that's what's happened now?"

She barely had to think about it.

"No," she said firmly. "Things are different now—a world away from where I was, before, physically, mentally...everything is so much better. I haven't been having so many nightmares, lately, and I haven't had a panic attack since that night at Nell's house. I know what I saw, Luke, and I saw a woman being pushed off that cliff, less than twenty minutes ago."

Luke walked around the counter to sit beside her, and took her hands between his own, to warm them.

"If you say that's what happened, then that's what happened."

She looked down to where their hands remained joined, and then up into his face.

"You believe me, then?"

He frowned. "Have a little faith, Gabi. What reason would I have to doubt you? You've been through a traumatising experience, but you've moved on since then. Besides," he said. "If a body has gone into the water, the chances are it'll wash up in the next few days, anyway."

She nodded, sombrely.

"I wonder who she was…"

"If she was local, we'll find out, soon enough," he said.

Now that the initial shock had passed, and the tea had thawed her body a bit, she became aware of her bedraggled state.

"God, I must look like some kind of sea urchin, and even they have standards."

For the first time, his lips twitched, and he lifted a hand to pluck out an errant twig from where it had become lodged in her hair.

"Why don't you have a warm shower, or even a bath? If you give me your clothes, I can stick them in the dryer, so they're ready when you come out?"

She was struck by a bittersweet thought.

His wife had been a lucky woman.

"What?" he asked her, reading the odd expression on her face.

"Nothing," she said, quietly. "I'd love that shower—thanks."

It wasn't just that she needed to wait around to see if DS Lander would call her with any news, it was that she wasn't ready to go home, alone, yet. The cove had shown her its darker side today, and the sea had given her a glimpse of its terrible power—both had left her wondering whether the paradise she'd imagined was no longer a paradise at all.

CHAPTER 20

Like everything in Luke's home, the master bathroom had been designed with an eye for form and function. Consequently, Gabrielle lounged in the giant copper bathtub for much longer than she'd intended, letting the water soothe her body and mind.

"Gabi? There's a call for you—it's Jane."

"I'll be there in a minute!"

Hoisting herself from the water with a mini tidal-wave of lavender-scented bubbles, she wound herself up in one of the fluffy white towels Luke had provided, stuffed her wet hair into another, and hurried back out into the living room to take the call.

"Hello?" she said, taking a seat next to Luke on the sofa.

"Hello, Gabi, this is DS Lander again," Jane said, obviously preferring to keep things on a professional standing when calling on official business.

"Yes—thank you for calling me back."

"I went out to Gull's Point, following the report you made. I'm afraid there was no sign of anybody by the time I got there, and there was no body on the rocks or in the sea below," she said. "However, as I said before, I've alerted the Coastguard, who will launch a vessel once conditions improve and it's safe to do so, and we'll continue to be vigilant to any sightings over the coming days."

Gabrielle didn't know what she'd expected, but she supposed a killer wouldn't choose to hang around the scene of a crime, waiting for the police to come and handcuff them.

"In the meantime, I'll need to take a formal statement from you," Jane continued. "Would tomorrow morning be convenient? The tide goes out at around five-forty-five, so I can be there at any time that suits you—although, after nine would certainly be preferable for me."

"Nine o'clock tomorrow morning is fine," Gabi said, and told her the address of her cottage, even though she must already have known.

"All right then," Jane said.

"Jane—ah, DS Lander? I wanted to ask, have there been any reports of missing persons?"

"It's too soon for that, I'd say," Jane replied. "It's been less than two hours since the incident, and it's usually the case that a family member or next of kin would only report a person formally 'missing' to the police when more time has passed, or they become seriously concerned."

Gabrielle made a sound of agreement. "Of course, that makes sense," she said.

Jane's voice softened. "Try not to worry, Gabi. We've done everything we can for the moment, and we'll be alert for any missing persons or bodies that wash up along the length of the shore."

"I wish there was something more I could do to help," she muttered.

"You've done enough," Jane said kindly, then advised her to try and get some sleep, and she'd see her the following morning.

After the call ended, Gabi was surprised to find that, once again, the weather had taken a mercurial turn. The storm clouds, which had come in so quickly, had gone again equally as swiftly, taking with them most of the heavy rain and leaving only a light dusting of moisture which clung to the plants in Luke's garden and dripped from the canopy above his veranda. The skies had mellowed to a clear amber-yellow and rays of sun danced across the water, which was now as gentle as a millpond.

"The sea is so unpredictable," she whispered. "One minute, it was as though Titan's wrath had befallen us all, and the next…"

Luke smiled.

"You get used to it," he said, and treated himself to a surreptitious glance at the smooth skin of her shoulders and neck, revealed above the line of the towel she still wore.

He cleared his throat. "I take it there were no developments?"

"None," she replied. "No sign of any body, nor of any smoking gun, as it were."

"That's not unexpected," he said. "There's a bad undercurrent at Gull's Point."

His words were spoken easily enough, but Gabrielle sensed a sudden tension in him that hadn't been there before.

"I'm sorry this has happened," she said. "For that poor woman, whoever she was. For myself, because a small, cowardly part of me wishes I hadn't been the one to see her fall. And, for you, Luke. I'm sorry if this whole thing brings back bad memories for you."

A muscle clenched in his jaw, and he looked away for a moment, thinking of what he wanted to say.

"I was going to tell you about what happened with Isobel," he said. "To be honest, I didn't want her ghost to dampen our…new friendship."

He turned back to look at her.

"When Isobel died, we hadn't been getting along," he said, bluntly. "I still loved her, but it wasn't the same as before. We'd argued a lot about what we both wanted from life and, frankly, it was different things. She was having second thoughts about living at the cove, whereas I loved the place and still do. She told me, out of the blue, that she didn't want to have children, whereas I've always hoped for a family, some day—"

Gabrielle listened with interest, because children was something she'd always hoped for, too. Her ideas about building a family had been a source of irritation to Mark, who preferred to be able to maintain his spontaneous life; to be able to go on expensive holidays whenever he liked and be able to lie-in on weekends. For her part, she'd believed that she'd loved him enough to want to have children together, to watch them grow and nurture the little family unit she'd always dreamed of. When Mark had told her that was his idea of a living hell, she'd been crushed.

"It's taken me two years of therapy to be able to admit that to myself, without feeling guilty," Luke continued. "We were fundamentally incompatible, but it was still no way for anyone to die."

His eyes darkened, as he remembered the last time he saw his wife, and it was something he wouldn't wish on another living soul.

"Drowning is a cruel, merciless death," he said. "I wouldn't wish it upon my worst enemy, and Isobel was very far from that."

Tears burned the back of Gabrielle's eyes while she listened to his heartfelt words, and she leaned forward, intending to kiss his cheek. Instead, he turned his head at the last moment and they both became very still, their eyes searching, until some silent message was exchanged, and their lips met—at first, tentatively, then more urgently.

When they parted, the towel on her head had been dislodged, and his fingers were speared through her wet hair.

"I can still walk you home," he said, softly. "These are hardly the best circumstances for a romantic Friday night in."

"I don't want to be alone, tonight," she said. "I was hoping you'd invite me to stay over, if only to sleep on your couch."

He smiled. "Oh, I think we can do a bit better than that."

Gabrielle only hoped she could remember how everything worked.

CHAPTER 21

To Gabrielle's great relief, it turned out that many things in life were just like riding a bike.

She'd fallen into an exhausted but contented sleep sometime during the early hours of the morning and, despite having every reason to suffer night terrors after having witnessed so patent a trigger, she slept peacefully until shortly after eight o'clock.

"Rise and shine," Luke said, softly.

She awakened to find him sitting next to her on his bed looking ruffled and gorgeous, already showered and dressed—much to her disappointment. Madge had slunk in sometime during the night and, after taking care of her morning ablutions, had returned to sleep in a large dog bed in the corner by the window, where she snored happily.

"I wanted to let you sleep, but Jane is due to be visiting your cottage at nine to take a statement—"

Of course, Gabi thought, with a stab of guilt. *How could she have forgotten?*

Instantly, the memory of what she'd seen yesterday came flooding back.

"Has there been any report in the local news? Anything at all?"

He waited until she'd dragged herself into a seated position, then handed her the cup of coffee he'd been holding.

"Nothing yet," he said. "But then, this is hardly the news capital of the world."

She took a sip of coffee, and almost purred.

In truth, she'd avoided drinking too much in the way of caffeinated drinks, on the advice of Doctor Chegwin, who'd said that it would be wise to steer clear of any dietary items that could exacerbate her anxiety disorders. Whilst she agreed with his advice up to a point, she wasn't ready to say 'goodbye' to one of life's greatest pleasures: savouring that first hit of coffee in the morning.

"This is almost better than—"

"Don't say, 'sex,'" he interjected. "My ego can't take that kind of rejection."

She giggled—actually *giggled*—and he grinned in return.

"I'm revising my opinion on that score, given recent experience," she said, and felt awash with guilt, once again.

There was a woman, somewhere out there, who'd never again know what it was like to share these moments, to laugh or drink coffee. It felt like bad taste to be revelling in those pleasures; almost as if she were dancing upon another woman's grave.

Luke sensed the sudden shift in her mood, and leaned forward to brush his lips against hers.

"You shouldn't feel sadness about being alive," he said. "You weren't responsible for that woman's death, Gabi."

She nodded, and turned her mind to practicalities.

"I'm supposed to be at the bookshop at nine-thirty, but I might be late, depending on how long it takes me to give Jane—DS Lander, that is—my statement," she said. "I haven't told Nell what happened, yet, so I'll need to give her a call."

"I can call and let her know, while you jump in the shower?" he offered.

Gabi thought that, if she wasn't careful, she could grow very used to having this man around. Then, Nell's words from the previous day popped into her mind…

There were a couple of women…nothing permanent, and nothing important.

She set her coffee cup down, feeling vulnerable.

"I'll leave you to get ready," he said, and called to the dog, who followed him with blind affection. Gabrielle had made that mistake once before, and was twice shy.

By the time nine o'clock rolled around, Gabi was back in her little cottage, pacing the kitchen floor while she awaited the arrival of DS Lander. With some dismay, she realised she'd stacked and unstacked, then re-stacked the small collection of books she had accumulated on the single bookcase in the living room, and had then scrubbed and re-scrubbed the kitchen table.

Once...
Twice...
A third time.

When there finally came a knock at the door at around nine-fifteen, she was feeling so taut with nerves, she needed to wait a full minute before answering, to be sure she had herself in full control.

"DS Lander? Thanks for coming over."

Jane Lander was dressed in civilian clothing, which consisted of jeans, a blouse and blazer combo, and a pair of smart, expensive-looking brown boots. All in all, she gave the impression of a middle-class woman who might just as easily have been coming over to give her some tips on interior design, rather than to discuss the grim topic of murder.

"Good morning," Jane replied, and produced her warrant card for inspection, which Gabi duly inspected before ushering her inside.

"Can I offer you some tea? Coffee?"

Jane shook her head. "That's kind of you but, no, I'm sure we're both eager to get straight down to business."

Gabrielle was relieved they were of the same mind, and gestured towards the sofa in the living room.

Once settled, Jane took out a notepad and a pen, scribbled the date and a few other pertinent details at the top, and then turned back to Gabrielle with a smile that was intended to put her at ease.

"Well, now," she said. "Let's start at the top, shall we?"

She listened patiently and without interruption while Gabrielle dictated her story, taking it all down and pausing only to ask the odd question here and there, particularly in respect of their unknown perpetrator and identifying features of the victim.

"You say the victim was female?" Jane said. "How can you be so sure?"

It wasn't the first time Gabi had been asked that question, so she was prepared.

"The hair, for one thing," she replied. "It was long and dark, and I saw it as…as she fell into the sea. Aside from that, there was something about her general stature as she stood on the cliff that definitely said 'female.'"

"Quite a few men—surf types, for example—wear their hair longer."

Gabi nodded. "I know," she said. "My instincts are still that she was a woman."

Jane made a note.

"In terms of stature, how did the victim's compare with the other figure—the perpetrator's—on the cliff-side? Was she taller or shorter? Did you get a good look?"

"I couldn't make out the details of either face; they were much too far away, and it was raining heavily," Gabrielle said. "But, in terms of height, I'd say the victim was marginally shorter than her perpetrator—perhaps half a head shorter?"

"All right," Jane murmured. "It doesn't help us now, since we don't know either of their identities, but if a body turns up it might give us a steer in finding the other person."

She looked up from her pad.

"Now, when you think back to that other person, and visualise them standing on the cliff, what do you see? Were they male or female?"

Gabrielle closed her eyes, to recall the memory.

"I couldn't tell you," she said, with frustration. "They wore a dark raincoat, something long, to the shins, with a big hood. It obscured most of their body, so I couldn't see what kind of clothing they were wearing or any of their features, really."

"Hmm," Jane said. "That kind of outerwear is very common in this part of the world. What about below the coat? Could you see bare legs, or trousers?"

Gabi thought back.

"Jeans, I think, although I couldn't be sure of the shade except they were dark—the rain would have darkened the material, though. The victim was wearing them, too, with a bright blue jacket."

"That should make her easier to spot," Jane said, laconically. "Now, coming back to the perp. Could you tell me their skin colour?"

Gabrielle started to reply in the negative, then remembered seeing their hands when they'd reached out to push the woman.

"White," she said, decisively. "They weren't wearing gloves when they pushed that woman."

Jane looked up at that.

"Any rings, or jewellery on the hands?"

"I couldn't make out that kind of detail," Gabrielle confessed.

Jane lifted a shoulder.

"It was worth a try," she said, and read back over the notes she'd just written. "All right, Gabi, I think I've got everything down. If you could read back over it, I'll type it up in the office later and send a copy through for you to sign."

Gabrielle nodded, twisting her hands tightly on her lap.

"What happens now? Have you heard anything else this morning?"

Jane sighed.

"I had another look over Gull's Point on my way here," she said. "Just in case there was anything in the way of tracks or trace evidence, but there was nothing. We still haven't found a body—the Coastguard took a boat out this morning to look, but no sign of anything untoward, so far."

"I've been told there's a bad undercurrent around there," Gabi said. "I suppose it's possible the body has been swept out to sea."

Jane seemed to consider her next words with care. "Gabi..." she began, and fiddled with the pen in her hand. "I should tell you that, whenever anyone new moves into the area, I do tend to do a standard background check."

She paused, to let that sink in.

"I see," Gabrielle said, and her eyes went flat. "You mean, you found out that I was a victim of the Tube Killer in London?"

Jane nodded. "That must have been harrowing for you," she said, sympathetically. "I completely understand why you experienced a panic attack at dinner, the other week, now that I know what happened to you. When Mike mentioned about the Tube Killer being apprehended, you went pale."

Gabrielle didn't bother to deny it.

"Do you have any more questions that would help you to find the person I saw, yesterday?" she said, tightly.

Jane sighed, and shook her head.

"Gabi, I don't want you to think that I don't take you seriously, because I do. Without any false modesty, I'm good at my job, and I follow up every single report that's made into my office. That being said, I also wanted to reassure you that, if it should happen to be the case that perhaps you made a *mistake*, there'll be no repercussions for any wasted time. We all understand and sympathise."

She offered her a kind smile, and Gabrielle realised that the woman meant well. Without any sign of a body and only the word of a traumatised crackpot to go on, DS Lander probably thought she would be helping to save any future embarrassment, when she, Gabi, naturally came to her senses and realised it had all been a terrible hallucination.

Except, it hadn't.

"Thank you," Gabrielle said, lifting her chin. "However, I can assure you that the report I've given is accurate in every respect, to the best of my knowledge. As much as I would rather I'd imagined the whole thing, detective sergeant, I can assure you that I know what I saw. I am an eyewitness to a murder, and they're somewhere out there, thinking they've got away with it. I won't let that happen."

Jane looked at her for a long moment, then nodded slowly.

"All right, then," she said. "I'll let you know if there are any developments in the coming days. In the meantime, take care of yourself."

"Why?"

"I won't be telling anyone about our conversation, because it's a matter of police business," Jane said. "However, as you already must know, the cove is a small place and word travels quickly. If someone *did* push a woman off those cliffs, and you're right about them thinking they've got away with it, they might not be too pleased to learn there was a witness to the crime."

"Oh, but it couldn't have been anyone who lives in the cove," Gabi said, happily. "When the tide comes in, nobody can get in or out except via the car park…"

"That's not strictly true," Jane said. "There's a set of very steep, very worn steps cut into the western cliffs which run up to Gull's Point. I shouldn't imagine anyone in their right mind would use them on a sunny day, let alone in the middle of a driving storm, but there's always the possibility."

Gabrielle was silent, considering the implications of that new snippet of information. Meanwhile, Jane reached into her pocket and pulled out a card with her number on it, which she set on the hallway table.

"This has all my numbers and my e-mail address on it," she said. "If you should ever need me, just call."

The door shut behind her, and Gabi rested her forehead on the wood, breathing slowly and deeply. There'd been a time when she'd have been so upset and so sensitive about her past history that she'd have been unable to string a sentence together to defend herself, or the wherewithal to show courage in her convictions.

She was making progress, every day.

CHAPTER 22

When Gabrielle made her way into work shortly after ten-thirty, Nell was ready and waiting with a mug of freshly-brewed coffee and a friendly ear.

"There you are!" she said, and rushed forward to envelop her in a bear-hug that, Gabrielle admitted, she had truly needed. "Luke told me what happened. Awful—just, awful! Come and sit yourself down…"

"Honestly, Nell, I'm fine," Gabi protested.

"You look like you've hardly slept," Nell said, her face full of concern. "All those bad memories it must have brought back for you."

If it wasn't for the genuine worry she read on her friend's face, Gabrielle might not have felt compelled to mention where she'd happened to spend the night, nor the more likely reason why she appeared not to have slept.

"You sly dawg," Nell declared, and threw back her head to let out one of her best and most wicked chuckles. "I *knew* you two would hit it off. I've got a sixth sense for these things. *Pat!*"

The lady stuck her head around the door.

"Did I hear my name?"

"You owe me a tenner, and a jar of macarons," Nell said.

Pat turned to Gabrielle, lifted a pencilled eyebrow and let out a little chuckle of her own.

"Well, well, well…this is nice."

"Anybody else?" Gabi wondered, throwing up her hands. "We could just sky-write it…"

Nell chose to ignore that remark.

"Well, now that we've established that you weren't in *quite* as bad a state as I'd feared, why don't you tell me how you're really doing?" she asked.

Gabi leaned back against her desk chair and considered the question.

"Yesterday, I was a bit shaken up," she admitted. "There were moments when I could feel my body succumbing to panic, but it didn't happen. I didn't *let* it happen."

"Good girl," Nell said, approvingly. "You're much stronger than you think. So what are the police doing about it?"

"Well, they've checked the whole of Gull's Point, but there's no sign of a body—or anyone at all, for that matter. Jane says she'll continue to follow it up, but I could tell she was sceptical. I mean, she knows what happened to me in London—a dark-haired woman of slight build, who was pushed almost to her death, with a known history of anxiety-related PTSD—and suddenly, here I am, claiming to have seen another dark-haired woman of slight build being pushed to her death. I don't blame her, really."

But Nell heard the resignation, and was sorry for it.

"If Jane says she'll follow it up, then she will," she said, firmly. "She might wonder about your past, but she's a decent woman, and she'd never let her own doubts or suspicions cloud an investigation, or even the possibility of one. You can rely on her to do the right thing."

Gabrielle nodded.

"She told me about the cliff stairs leading up to Gull's Point," she said, uneasily.

"Jacob's Ladder? That's what we call them, around here. I didn't mention them, before, because they've been designated unsafe for use for the past ten years or more. Nobody around here uses them, now. What about them?"

"Nothing," Gabi mumbled. "That's a relief, anyway."

Everyone in the cove was kind and sympathetic, but Gabrielle was sure she sensed a certain look behind their eyes; the kind of hesitant, 'careful-not-to-hurt-her-feelings' sort of look she'd seen from all her colleagues back at Frenchman Saunders, after the fall. If she'd been half as paranoid as she was, back then, she'd have imagined them whispering about her, and wondering whether she'd made the whole thing up.

Perhaps, they still were—the only difference was, she didn't care so much anymore.

Instead, she carried on, trying not to allow her eyes to stray across to the cliff where she'd seen it happen, or to think about what could wash up on the sand and spoil somebody's day. She heard from her friend, Frenchie, to say that Saffron Wallows would be completing a book tour during the first week of September and would be happy to include Carnance Books on her list of places to visit, which, in turn, gave Gabrielle the idea of hosting their Grand Re-Opening Party on the same evening, so they could really make a splash, so to speak. To that end, she made a long list of people to invite: local authors, those from further afield, fellow booksellers, distributors, local press outlets and, of course, readers, who were the most important of all.

Once that was done, she turned her mind to the other bits of admin she'd been avoiding, and was irritated to find that a number of rejection e-mails she'd sent out to the various people who'd applied for the position Amy had vacated were still sitting in her outbox, having failed to send.

"Bloody internet," she surmised, and tried to re-send.

Server error.

Swearing softly, she picked up her phone and decided to phone each one, in turn, as a matter of courtesy. It might take half an hour, but it was the right thing to do.

Twenty minutes later, she'd spoken to each of the applicants, bar one, who was the last on her list.

Tamsyn Bray.

She dialled the number given at the top of her CV, but it didn't ring, and soon after an automated message came through to say that the number was no longer available.

Gabi set the phone back down on the desk and sat there for a moment or two, tapping the tips of her index fingers together. There was no reason to draw any conclusions from that, considering many people ended up losing or damaging their phones, or simply changing their number without updating everyone as to the new one.

Shrugging it off, she moved on to the next job on her list, which managed to occupy her for all of two minutes, before she abandoned it, in favour of seeking out Tamsyn Bray via social media.

She'd try one more time, then leave it at that.

Bringing up Facebook, Gabrielle typed in the name and scrolled through a list of four or five 'Tamsyn Brays', until she found the one that she was looking for, from Ruan Minor, only a few miles from where she now sat. The privacy settings were not set too high on the account, so she was allowed to send a message, which she began typing in the hope that it would be received:

Dear Tamsyn,

Thank you for your recent application to Carnance Books & Gifts for the position of Summer Customer Service Staff. Unfortunately, on this occasion, your application was not successful. However, I wanted to get in touch to thank you for taking the time to apply, and to ask if we might keep your CV on record for a while longer, in case another position should come up?

Many thanks,
Gabrielle Adams (Manager)

P.S. Apologies for contacting you directly via social media—unfortunately, I was unable to contact you via telephone today, as it appears to have been disconnected, and we are having some trouble with our e-mail server.

After sending the message, Gabrielle scrolled back up to the top of Tamsyn's page, where there was a profile picture, and clicked to enlarge it. Instantly, an image of a pretty girl of around twenty or twenty-one popped up, showing her smiling into the camera with the beach at her back. She was wearing classic beach garb: denim cut-offs, a teeny-tiny black crop top which showcased a perfectly flat, tanned stomach beneath, and a long, handmade pendant with a shell woven onto the end of it was hanging from her neck. She also happened to have very long, very dark hair.

A pounding began in the base of Gabrielle's skull, and with a trembling finger, she began to scroll down the page, where she saw a couple of messages from Tamsyn's friends:

Missed you, last night! What happened? Something's wrong with your phone xoxo and:

Are you coming to Sky Bar next weekend? Ed says plz can you let him know so he can sort out tickets. Did you get my text btw? Need to know how it went on Thursday night ;)

Gabi told herself she was clearly over-reacting. She was frustrated because the police doubted her credibility as a witness, and so she was obviously trying to discover the identity of the victim, to prove herself to them and to everyone else—that was all. That was no good reason to start imagining that every dark-haired young woman she happened to come across might be the missing link.

And yet...

Two of this girl's friends were querying where she was, and had mentioned they were having similar problems contacting her by phone.

Long, dark hair...

CHAPTER 23

There was no more time to dwell on the matter of Tamsyn Bray, because her help was soon required to deal with an endless flow of lunchtime customers seeking shelter from the heat of the midday sun. Luke was one of them, and the sight of him waiting patiently in the counter queue looking tall and tanned brought a little leap to her heart, which was something she'd have to think about later.

"Do you have a lunch break coming up?" he asked, when they were eye to eye. "I thought we could have a picnic on the beach."

"Not for another—"

"She can take a break now," Nell's voice interrupted, from the other end of the counter. "Elena! Come and take over from Gabi."

Gabrielle acquiesced because, really, it was a generous thing for Nell to do, and she'd have been churlish to refuse.

"In that case, I'll have one of the picnic hampers for two," Luke said, with a smile.

Soon after, they strolled down to the sand and picked their way through the small camps of people who had carved out a little area for themselves on the beach, in search of one of their own.

"Where's Madge?"

"I left her snoring in her bed," he said. "She prefers to walk in the early evening, when the crowds have died down."

Gabi nodded, and decided she agreed with her.

"Doesn't it feel strange, having to share the beach with outsiders?" Gabrielle asked him. "I find myself feeling a little bit territorial."

"Spoken like a true outsider," he teased her. "But, yes, it does, sometimes. I have to remind myself that the cove isn't mine alone. It's everyone's."

"If anybody's, it must surely be Nell's?"

"I don't think she'd agree with you," he said. "Nell sees herself as a sort of custodian of the cove, nothing more. She makes sure it's looked after, that there's no rubbish or anything like that. I think it makes her happy to share such a beautiful place with others."

"Well, now I just feel bad," she said, and he turned to her with a laugh.

"You're helping her do that, you know. Building the books side to her business will attract more people, and bring more trade to the other small businesses here and in Luddo."

Gabrielle nodded, and followed him around the curve of the eastern headland towards a secluded spot in the sand.

"Will this do?" he asked.

She smiled, knowing he'd deliberately veered away from the western headland so that she would not be reminded of what happened the day before. There was little to prevent the incident occupying her thoughts, but it was good of him to try.

They seated themselves on the soft sand and she was content to look out at the rippling waves while he unwrapped their food.

"How did it go this morning?" he asked, once they'd tucked in.

"As well as it could," she said. "I told Jane everything, and she promised to follow it up, which she's already done."

"But—?"

"But what?"

"I sensed a 'but' coming," he said, and took a bite of homity pie.

Gabrielle shrugged.

"Jane also told me that, if it turned out that I'd made a mistake, that would be fine, and everyone would understand. Jude told me much the same thing, and Pat's been clucking around, all day, asking if I'm feeling all right and just to let her know if I feel faint again. They haven't done that since the night I had the panic attack, so it's obvious they think I've lost the plot."

"They might equally think you've been dreadfully unlucky and in need of a friend," Luke pointed out.

"But I hear what you're saying. You've come a long way, since London, and it's a kick in the teeth for anybody to doubt your word."

"There was a time when nobody would have questioned it," she said, and began drawing circles in the sand. "Do you?"

"Do I—?"

"Do you believe me?"

"Yes, Gabi, I believe you. Do you believe yourself?"

She looked up with troubled eyes.

"Yes, but the more I think about it, the more I start to doubt myself."

"Maybe you think too much," he said, with devastating logic.

She stared at him, then began to laugh.

"You really are the most infuriating person," she said.

"That wasn't what you were saying last night," he replied, quick as you like.

And, before she could think of a suitably witty riposte, he'd closed the gap between them and lowered his lips to hers for a thorough kiss.

"You play dirty," she told him, when his head lifted again.

"That's just the start of it," he replied. "What are you doing this evening?"

She couldn't think of anything she'd rather be doing than spending it with him, and she said as much.

"I thought I could paint you," he said, casually.

She almost dropped the pie she was holding.

"Paint me? No...you don't want to do that."

"Why not? You'd be a wonderful subject."

"I—for one thing—I—" She scrambled about for an excuse, but could find none. "I've never been painted before."

"There's a first time for everything," he said. "How about this: if you don't enjoy the process, we'll stop right away. If you don't like the painting at the end, we'll get rid of it."

"That sounds fair," she acknowledged. "Do I get to keep it?"

"Nope," he said, with a laugh. "This one's for me. But you can choose another painting, as a fair exchange. How does that sound?"

They shook on it, and talk turned to other things.

"I haven't seen much of Jack, lately," Gabrielle remarked, spotting him out on the water with a group of paddle-boarders. "I wonder where he's been hiding himself."

Luke made an expressive face.

"Stick a pin in a map, and you'll probably be close," he said, and she gave him a playful nudge in the ribs.

"He's really not so bad," she said. "Underneath all the flirting and the vanity, he's a man who loves his mother to distraction, and doesn't like to stray too far from her."

"And woe betide the woman who does eventually take him from her," Luke remarked. "They'd have to be something special, or they simply wouldn't make the grade."

"They must have been so close, growing up," Gabi said, thinking of what Nell had told her about the early days, when she'd had very little to her name. "There was no father figure on the scene, so it's always been Jackson and Nell."

Luke nodded, narrowing his eyes as he watched Jackson paddle towards a pretty girl of nineteen or twenty, having chosen her as the pick of the bunch.

"Nell made sure he never wanted for anything," he said, with a note of affection. "But there's a dark side to that, don't you think? If you're somebody who's been born with looks, charm and the rest, and have grown used to having your way, what would that somebody do, if they were ever told 'no'?"

"Have a tantrum?" she suggested, and he laughed.

"You're probably right."

But still, his eyes strayed to where the other man frolicked in the water, and he wondered.

CHAPTER 24

The remainder of the weekend passed by in a happy blur of beach walks, al fresco dinners and steamy evenings, rounded off by a wonderful day spent on the north side of Cornwall's western peninsula, in St Ives, where Luke was happy to show Gabrielle around the gallery he owned overlooking the harbour. It was the perfect spot for passing trade, and she saw a different side to the man she'd come to know at the cove; outside of it, he was urbane and business-savvy, polite and friendly with his staff, who seemed to be on very good terms with him.

As for the art...

On every wall, there was something to capture the imagination—be it a painting in watercolour or a piece of pottery—and he'd practically been forced to drag her away. They'd pottered around the little shops, she'd popped into another bookshop on one of the little town's cobbled streets and chatted with the owner, taking the time to invite them to the party at the end of the summer, and ended the day with dinner at a restaurant right on the beach, beneath the stars. She'd enjoyed three solid nights of sleeping without nightmares, and felt completely rejuvenated.

Despite all that, Gabrielle checked the news reports every day for word of a body having washed up, but there was none that fitted the bill, and as time wore on, she began to wonder if she'd been wrong, after all.

However, when Monday rolled around once more and she found herself at her desk in the back office of Carnance Books, Gabrielle's fingers itched to check the Facebook profile page of Tamsyn Bray. Remembering the message she'd sent a couple of days before, she decided to log in and check to see if there'd been a response.

Just following up, she told herself. *Nothing wrong with that.*

But when she logged into the account, she could see that the message remained unread. What was more, there had been three more messages left by her friends asking what had become of her, since the last time she'd checked.

Gabrielle felt the hairs on the back of her neck begin to prickle as she looked into the silent, staring eyes of the dark-haired girl, and she began to reach for her phone, intending to call DS Lander and tell her all about it.

Then, she stopped herself.

Jane already thought she was a couple of sandwiches short of a picnic, and would probably say she needed to step back and allow the police to do their work. After all, no missing persons report had been made—which was another thing she'd been checking every day—and, with no body and no other witnesses, she didn't want to waste their time if this thing with Tamsyn Bray turned out to be a false lead.

Then, it struck her.

Tamsyn had given her address on the covering letter of her CV, so Gabi fished it out of the folder she'd filed away.

Caravan 78
Paradise Holiday Park
Luddo Fields

Gabrielle had passed the holiday park once or twice when she'd taken a trip into Luddo, and knew exactly where it was. If she happened to be passing, where would be the harm in stopping by to see the girl? There would be no harm at all, since she'd be hand-delivering a response to a job application that hadn't otherwise been received. Nobody would need to know about it, because all Gabrielle wanted to do was see the girl for herself, in the flesh, and then leave.

Nobody needed to know.

Unless, of course, the girl called Tamsyn Bray was already dead.

By the evening, Gabrielle was decided on the matter.

The tide wasn't due to roll into the cove until late, after midnight, which gave her plenty of time to take her bike into Luddo and pay Tamsyn Bray a visit. The timing worked well, because Luke had already told her he would be away for a night in London, on business, not returning until the following afternoon. That saved any embarrassing explanations about her need to play Inspector Clouseau, and she could satisfy herself with an answer, once and for all.

After locking up the shop shortly after six, Gabi joined the dregs of the beach crowd and made her way up the beach path towards the car park, where she'd found a handy spot to lock up her bike, beside one of the old bird-watching huts that faced the sea. Wrapping up in a summer jacket, to stave off the evening chill, she pedalled swiftly towards Luddo before she could change her mind.

The caravan park was large and sprawling, on the far side of the village. At some point, a farmer had sold off their land, which was now occupied by rows of ageing cream and white fixed caravans, some of which sported striped canopies and extensions to allow for outdoor dining. As she entered the park, she was met with the overpowering scent of smoke and barbecued meat, and she dismounted to push the bike slowly along the rows in search of the number she was looking for.

It took Gabrielle ten minutes to reach Caravan 78, for it was in the far corner of the caravan park away from the main entrance, beneath the shaded branches of a large, overgrown tree. It was, clearly, one of the less desirable spots, and the caravan itself appeared to have been rarely used—or cleaned, for that matter. There were no signs of life at the caravans either side of it, the barbecues and outdoor parties having petered out several rows hence.

At first glance, the caravan appeared to be unoccupied. There were no lights at its windows, and no wellies or coats hanging up from a peg outside. All the same, Gabi did what she had set out to do, and rested her bike on the ground before approaching the front door to knock.

No answer.

Peering through the mottled, porthole window on the front door, she could see the hazy outline of a tiny kitchen, a bench and table, but no people within.

She knocked again, louder this time.

Still, no answer.

Feeling a rising sense of panic, Gabrielle stepped away from the front door and, looking in either direction, moved around to the side, to see if she could get a better view of the interior from one of the windows. But, after completing a full circle of the caravan, she could see nothing within.

She might be out, a rational voice whispered.

Or she might be dead, another voice replied.

Gabi hovered in the gathering twilight, and then, with a muttered expletive, surged forward to try the front door.

Miraculously, it swung open.

Nobody locks their front doors around here, Nell had said, and it turned out that she was right.

Inside the caravan, all was dim and smelled slightly of decaying bananas and old milk.

"Hello?" Gabi called out. "Is anybody home?"

There came no reply, just as she had expected.

She wavered for a moment, knowing she should turn back, but found herself walking forward instead, peering through the cramped, shadowed interior looking for any signs of habitation.

. And there were plenty.

Dry laundry hung over the back of a small clothes rack which stood to one side, displaying tiny lace knickers and a black bra, alongside a couple of t-shirts with motifs on the front. On the table, there was a single apple left in a wooden bowl, now turning brown with age, attracting fruit flies which circled above it like tiny vultures. On the kitchen counter there was a couple of brown envelopes and she saw they were both addressed to Tamsyn Bray, and had been redirected to that address from somewhere else. She couldn't see the old address without peeling off the sticker, and even she was not bold enough to tamper with evidence. There were no electronics, nor any sign of a mobile phone.

Now that she'd confirmed that the girl did live there, but clearly hadn't been back in a couple of days, Gabi knew she should leave—and leave, quickly.

But she saw the bedroom door was ajar, and she had to know.

She had to check…

She edged it open with the tip of her elbow and it swung back on squeaking hinges to reveal—

"*Gabi?*"

She let out a blood-curdling scream and fell back against the elm wood door, eyes wide with terror.

"J—DS Lander," she said, as the woman stepped into the caravan and removed her sunglasses. "I didn't hear you."

"Obviously," Jane said, with more than a touch of irritation. "I had a report about an intruder sniffing around, but I never imagined it would be *you*. What on Earth do you think you're doing?"

Gabrielle knew there would be no point in trying to talk herself out of this one. She'd gone too far, with her amateur sleuthing, and there was every chance she'd be in real trouble now.

Swallowing back the kind of fear that came with having been a law-abiding citizen her whole life, she stepped away from the bedroom door and laid her cards out on the table.

"I'm here because the girl—the woman who lives here, applied for a job at the bookshop," she said. "Her name is Tamsyn Bray. I tried to contact her to let her know she hadn't been successful with the job application, but couldn't get through to her, so I tried to contact her through social media, thinking that would be quicker—"

"That's an awful lot of effort for an unsuccessful applicant," Jane was bound to say.

Gabi swallowed.

"Well—yes, I suppose so. But the thing is, when I went to send her a message on Facebook, I happened to see that several of her friends were wondering where she'd got to, and they're all saying her mobile phone isn't working, which is exactly the problem I found."

"What are you trying to tell me, Gabi?"

"I think this girl might be missing," she replied. "And there's more. The girl has long, dark hair—"

Jane heaved a sigh, and shook her head.

"I'm surprised at you," Jane said, managing to scold her as well as her own mother might have done. "Gabi, I don't need to tell you that breaking and entering is a criminal offence. It's customary not to enter another person's property without their permission."

"I understand that," she replied. "And, believe me, if I hadn't been worried about the girl's whereabouts, I wouldn't have—it's just that the door was unlocked…"

"It isn't up to you to do the work of the police," Jane said, fairly. "If you had concerns about this girl, you should have called me, or one of my staff, as I asked you to."

Now, her voice was tinged with hurt.

"I know I'm just a copper from the regions, and I've been off work on maternity leave, but that doesn't mean I can't do my job."

Gabrielle couldn't have felt worse if she'd tried. She had been so wrapped up in her own search for the truth, she hadn't considered others she might be hurting in the process.

"I'm sorry," she said. "I really am. I should have rung you straight away, as soon as I began to have concerns about Tamsyn. I can assure you, Jane, it has nothing to do with me thinking you're not capable in any way."

Jane pursed her lips, and let out a long sigh.

"So, you say this girl seems to be AWOL? When did you send her a message on social media?"

"On Monday," Gabi replied, eager to be as helpful as possible. "You can read it, if you like."

"I'll need you to send through screenshots of the messages," Jane agreed. "Did you receive any reply?"

"No, as I say, I don't think the message has even been read. From the messages I can see on her timeline, I don't think her friends have heard from her, either."

Jane nodded, and glanced around the caravan, before indicating that they should leave.

"Aren't you going to search the place?"

Jane rolled her eyes heavenward.

"*No*, Gabi, because, as a police officer, I'm bound by the rules of the Police and Criminal Evidence Act. That means, no barging into people's homes without a search warrant, for one thing."

"But isn't there an exemption, if you're investigating murder?"

"There is, clever clogs, but you have to make a causal link between the two and—without wishing to be rude—hearsay evidence passed along the grapevine doesn't cut it. If, once I've had a chance to look into this woman's whereabouts, I come to the same conclusions you have, then I'll come back and conduct a proper search through the proper channels. Until that time, think yourself bloody lucky I'm not issuing you with a caution."

Gabrielle nodded, as meekly as she could.

"Thank you. But you're going to look into it—"

"Yes," Jane said. "But I'm ninety-nine percent sure this—what was her name? Tamsyn?"

"Tamsyn Bray."

"Right. Well, she's probably off partying with friends, or something of that kind. Chances are, she's over at Watergate Bay toasting marshmallows on the beach or smoking weed, with the rest of them."

Gabi wasn't convinced, but she knew when to call it quits.

"Thank you for being so understanding," she said.

"My understanding has limits," Jane said, seriously. "Please, don't ever put me in a position like this again."

CHAPTER 25

It was dark by the time Gabrielle returned to the cove.

Her first inclination was to wander up the hill to see Luke, before remembering that he was away in London. The thought left her feeling oddly bereft, and then irritated by her own growing sense of attachment to someone she'd known for such a short space of time.

She turned the thought over in her mind as she let herself into her cottage, and went through the automatic motions of checking all the little traps she left for potential intruders. It was a habit she hadn't felt ready to abandon, although things were steadily improving, otherwise—that very morning, she'd left the soap facing in the wrong direction, and had washed her hands twice, rather than the three times she'd relied upon for the past six months.

It was a good start.

Gabi wandered around the house checking the locks, checking the hair she'd sellotaped to the edge of a closed door, and all the other silly little booby-traps she'd spent half an hour setting up. She was pleased to see that everything was as she'd left it.

Except for one thing.

Entering the kitchen, she looked at the dining chair she'd propped up against the back door, and her skin broke out in goosepimples. The two balancing legs of the chair were always placed in exactly the same spot on the tiled floor, whilst still allowing the wooden upright to tuck underneath the handle of the back door and block entry for any intruder who planned to try and force the lock.

Now, the legs were two inches out of place, and the angle of the chair much wider than usual.

It had been moved.

Her vision blurred, and Gabi hurried over to check the lock, which appeared to be intact, but it didn't remove the plain and simple fact that the chair was not where she'd left it.

Somebody had been inside the house.

She backed away from the door, eyes dilated as she traced every inch of the kitchen to seek out any other minute alterations. Finding none, she moved into the hallway and looked upstairs, feeling the blood pounding in her ears while her chest rose and fell.

In her peripheral vision, she caught sight of the knife block, and moved swiftly to grasp one of the carving knives in her hand before returning to the stairs.

"Is—is anybody there?" she called out.

She felt stupid, calling out something so obvious. What did she expect them to say?

Oh, yes, it's me, the clifftop killer from the other day—I'll be right down!

She let out a hissing breath between her teeth and told herself, firmly, to get a grip—which she did, one hand curling around the bannister while the other continued to grip the handle of the knife she held at her side. Then, she moved slowly up the stairs, hearing the soft creak of her own footsteps as she neared the landing. Her eyes roamed up and down, in case she was surprised from behind, her body on high alert.

There were only four rooms upstairs, and she took each of them in turn, beginning with the nearest. It happened to be the spare bedroom, which she searched quickly, beneath the bed and inside the narrow wardrobe that was built into one of the eaves.

Nothing.

Next came the family bathroom, which she only used for bathing, since it had the freestanding bath she enjoyed so much.

Nothing.

Finally, the master bedroom and small en-suite shower room. She slid into the room, keeping her back to the wall, and reached for the light switch, turning it on with a flourish. At first glance, the room appeared to be just as she'd left it, except for one important feature.

The book.

Saffron Wallows' book, which she'd finished reading a few days before, had been taken from the shelf where she'd placed it, alphabetically, downstairs, and was now sitting on her bedside table. Drawn to it, Gabi moved forward, her breathing short and unsteady, until it was within reach.

She almost grasped it, before remembering there might be evidence worth preserving, and took a moment to tug down the cuff of her jumper to use as a makeshift glove. With it, she turned the book over and saw that several pages had been turned down, which was another thing she never did, as a lifelong bibliophile.

That's what bookmarks were for...

Moving past that, admittedly, minor infraction, she opened the pages that had been marked, and then sank onto the edge of the bed with a sob.

Several passages had been circled in red, with enough force to bleed through the pages. Those passages came from some of the most harrowing parts of the storyline, where its protagonist was on the verge of suicide:

I asked myself, time and again, why I was still alive...what good did I bring to the world?

and:

I knew there were ways to end it all, if I really wanted to. If it came to it, I could hurl myself off a cliff...

The book fell to the floor and Gabi covered her face with both hands as tears began to fall, her breath hitching as she tried to control the hysteria which threatened to engulf her mind. She rose from the bed, moving blindly to the adjoining en-suite in search of a beta-blocker, catching sight of her own face in the mirror.

She looked lost, was her first thought. *Completely lost.*

Shaking, scrubbing the tears from her eyes with an angry hand, she made a grab for the little bottle of pills she kept in the cabinet above the sink, for emergency use. She'd never taken to relying on them, being of the mindset that she would take prescribed drugs when necessary but *only* when necessary, to avoid any kind of addiction. After a long talk with Doctor Chegwin and her psychiatrist, back in London, she'd agreed a staged withdrawal from the anti-depressants and likewise the anti-anxiety drugs.

It should therefore have been the case that the little bottle of beta-blockers was almost full, but instead she found the bottle completely empty.

"What—?" she muttered.

She snatched open the cupboard again and checked its contents, looking to find an identical bottle, in case she'd forgotten to throw an old one away.

There was no other bottle; only that one.

Gabi looked down at the little brown bottle with its clinical label and then set it down on the edge of the sink, moving away from it with extreme caution.

Where had all the pills gone?

Had she taken them all?

She couldn't remember. Just like so many things, she couldn't remember.

CHAPTER 26

Gabrielle ran out of the house and up the hill to Nell's place, clutching the little bottle of empty pills in her hand. She didn't stop to think of the time, or how she might have looked, but went straight to a place she believed to be safe and banged loudly on the door.

"All right! All right! I'm coming!"

Nell's voice filtered through the wood and then, a moment later, she appeared in the doorway dressed in striped, Turkish-style pyjamas.

"Gabi? What's the matter? What's happened?"

She took one look at her face, which was filled with fear, and tugged her inside.

"Come with me," she said. "Jackson! Get in here! We've got trouble!"

A moment later, he hurried into the living room wearing nothing but a pair of boxer shorts.

"For God's sake," Nell muttered, but turned to focus her attention on Gabrielle, who was seated on the extreme edge of the sofa and looked as though she'd just seen Caesar's ghost.

"They'd moved the chair," she blurted out.

Nell and Jackson exchanged a perplexed glance.

"Chair? What chair, and who moved it?"

"I don't know who," Gabi said, twisting the bottle in her hands. "I just know that, when I got back to the cottage, it had been moved from underneath the door."

"You...you've been using a chair to bar the door?" Nell asked, with a note of sadness. "Is that what you mean?"

"Yes, yes," Gabi said, impatiently, and told herself to remain calm. Just get the words out. "After the fall—my fall, not...not the other woman's—I felt very unsafe. I developed some OCD habits to help me to control the fear."

"All right," Nell said, coming to sit down beside her. "That's understandable."

"I'd have hired a bodyguard," Jackson said, with a grin.

Gabi managed a small smile in return.

"Tonight, the chair legs were in the wrong place. I know, because I always put them in the same place. And then, there was the book…"

She continued to twist the empty bottle in her hands, and Jackson frowned.

"Gabi—did you take all those pills?" he asked, and looked over at his mother, whose expression shifted to instant concern.

"These—no, no, I don't think so," she said. "It's another thing they did—"

"You don't *think* so, or you *know* you didn't take them, Gabi?" Nell asked her, cutting to what she considered to be the heart of the matter.

"I—" Tears welled up again, because she wanted to say that she was positively certain she hadn't, but she was so upset by the chain of events that she couldn't trust her own memory anymore. "I'm almost sure."

"Gabi, I'm sorry, but I need to call Doctor Chegwin if you're not certain—we need to get you to a hospital—"

Later, Gabrielle would think that her friend's suggestion was entirely to her credit but, at that moment, it was only a source of further emotional turmoil.

"You don't understand," she said, miserably. "I came back from the caravan park to find someone had been in my house—I'm certain of it. The chair had been moved, as I said, the book I'd been reading has been marked up in red, with passages on suicide circled for me to find. Then, when I went into the bathroom, I found this bottle completely empty. I *know* I didn't take them all, Nell. I wouldn't do that."

It was a lot to take in.

"Why were you at a caravan park?" Jackson asked, and his mother turned to him with a look bordering on despair, as if to say, 'of all the things, that's what you're worrying about?'

"I think I've found the missing girl, the one who was pushed off the cliff," Gabi replied, softly. "I didn't want to tell anyone, at first, in case I was wrong. But now, I feel certain it's her."

She explained what had happened, and why she felt so sure.

"You're bloody lucky Jane didn't caution you for that," Jackson exclaimed, after she'd finished telling the tale. "She's a stickler for the rules."

"And she's been doing her job," Nell added quietly. "She's asked each of us where we were, at the time in question."

Gabrielle hadn't realised. "She has? That's something…"

Nell raised an eyebrow. "No, no, I don't mean it's because I expect you have anything to hide," Gabi amended. "It's just good to know she's taking me seriously."

She only wished she could ask them herself, without sounding completely paranoid.

"It's the other things I'm concerned about. A chair leg could have been dislodged, at a stretch," Nell said thoughtfully. "But the book with red marker pen—and the pill bottle? That's very deliberate."

"You believe me, then? You don't think I did these things myself?"

"You've had days—*weeks* to start messing with your own mind, if you'd wanted to," Nell said. "Why start now, when you've been happier than ever, and with a future to look forward to?"

She was right, Gabi thought. She hadn't been dwelling on the past, as she had a few months ago. The intrusive thoughts had been far less frequent, and she hadn't harboured any truly low thoughts since she'd been in hospital or during the immediate aftermath of her ordeal.

The timing made no sense.

"But how would anyone manage to get into the cottage?" she asked. "I always lock the doors, unlike the rest of Cornwall."

Nell sighed, and ran a hand through her hair.

"I'm to blame for that," she said. "Most people would know I keep a locked box full of keys for the cottages, the bookshop, the surf shack and whatnot. Easy enough to figure out the key code, or swipe a key, when nobody's around. It'd have to be someone local, though."

"Pat and Jude have a key," Jackson put in. "Jude does the maintenance work on the properties around the cove, so he keeps a set of keys for access during emergencies, in case there's a plumbing leak, or something like that. If they didn't want to try and jimmy your locked box, Mum, they could have walked straight into Pat and Jude's and found a key in there."

"That's true," she said, and blamed herself even more.

"It had to have happened sometime today, or last night, after seven," Gabrielle said, thinking through the processes. "I was with Luke after then, and didn't get back home until just after eight-thirty, this evening."

"That leaves a fairly open window," Nell said. "The tide didn't come in until almost midnight, last night, which leaves almost five hours during which someone could have snuck inside and tampered with your things. Equally, the tide went out at around six o'clock this morning, so that left somebody all day today."

"How could they have known where you'd be?" Jackson wondered aloud, and unwittingly preyed upon the single most terrifying feature in all of it.

"Because they're not a stranger," Gabi said, very quietly. "Whoever did this to me, to frighten me and make me doubt my own sanity, knows me and knows my habits. They know I've been spending time with Luke in the evenings and that I work at the bookshop during the day."

"The work rota is up on the kitchen wall," Nell said, unhappily. "Anyone who goes in there would be able to see it."

But who?

Who?

Gabrielle looked between their faces, which were twin masks of concern, and felt a sudden chill.

She came to her feet.

"Thank you so much for listening to my ravings," she said. "I think—I need to go home now. It's been quite a day."

Nell was surprised.

"Why don't you stay with us tonight, love? Surely, you won't want to go back to the cottage, now? Besides, don't you want to ask Jane to come and have the place fingerprinted, in case the bastard—whoever they are—left something behind?"

Gabrielle knew the police would find nothing, so it became a question of whether her fear of being alone at the cottage outweighed her fear of staying with Nell and Jackson.

There was a third choice, she realised, and she hoped that he wouldn't mind.

CHAPTER 27

The storm raged all around, rain slicing at her skin like a thousand icy darts while the wind rushed over the cliffs to nudge at her back, as if it were encouraging her to go on...do it...push...

What's the matter, Gabi?

Why are you looking at me like that?

You know why...

You've always wanted what was mine.

Still, the wind nudged her onward, whistling in her ear.

Push...push...push...

I'm sorry, Gabi. I'm so sorry. I never meant for it to happen.

Liar.

She felt her legs move forward, inch by inch, of their own volition.

What are you doing?

What I should have done a long time, ago. I'm cutting you loose, Frenchie.

As a bolt of lightning struck, crackling through the sky like a whip, she saw her friend's face.

Push…push…push…

PUSH!

Her arms lifted and she lunged, throwing her weight forward until her hands connected with her friend's chest, propelling her backward and over the edge of the cliff. She watched Frenchie's face form an 'o' of shock and surprise, her long hair flying after her like a severed rope…

Gabrielle awoke with a scream, her arms and legs thrashing against the bedclothes, her body drenched with sweat. In the darkness of Luke's bedroom, she could still picture Frenchie's mouth opened wide as she slipped backward into the sea, and she reached across to turn on the side light to try to dispel any last remaining vestiges of the nightmarish image.

After leaving Nell's house, she'd packed a few things into a bag and walked up the pathway to Luke's place, thankful that there were solar powered lights to guide the way, or else she could have done herself an injury. As soon as she'd regained mobile reception, she'd sent him a message and hoped he wasn't already asleep.

He'd replied immediately.

Stay as long as you need—keys are under the blue plant pot. Madge is with me, so no dog to surprise you at the door. See you tomorrow x

It had felt strange, at first, moving around a house that was not hers, turning on lights and filling a kettle that was not her own, but she was comforted by the familiarity, and it was infinitely preferable to spending the night alone in the cottage, after an intruder had invaded her privacy so thoroughly.

There, in the semi-darkness of the early dawn, Gabrielle thought again of the nightmare she'd just had, and of what it might mean. She often had repetitive nightmares that were more like relived memories of real-life events, sometimes tweaked here and there, but broadly just uncomfortable and distressing reminders of things that had already happened and which she could not change. But, in the dream she'd just had, she'd experienced the murder of a woman—in this case, her friend—from the killer's perspective, and in circumstances similar to those she'd so recently witnessed.

The question was, then: why would she wish to kill Frenchie?

To her knowledge, she had no reason to bear her any animosity, so what possible reason should she have to imagine her dead?

I never meant for it to happen, Frenchie had said, in the nightmare.

Was that a figment of her imagination, Gabi wondered, or one of the suppressed memories that occasionally came back to her, over the course of time?

It was impossible to say.

But if it was a memory, what was it that Frenchie had never meant to happen?

When Gabrielle went to work later that morning, it was with the express intention of not breathing a word about what had happened the previous day or showing any sign that it had affected her. If there was somebody out there who wished her harm, or hoped to undermine her self-belief, she wanted to send a clear signal that they'd failed. She was still there, and would be for a very long time, no matter what they tried to do.

The pill box had been bad, Gabrielle was forced to admit, but marking up Saffron's book was much worse, and it had been there that the unknown intruder had made a catastrophic error in judgment. For, whilst she might have been persuaded to believe that she'd tampered with her own pills, there was no way that Gabi would ever have drawn all over a book, no matter what her mental state might feasibly have been.

It was just too implausible.

If the intention was to have her believe that she was thinking of suicide, and that she was losing her memory again, then they'd failed to achieve their goal. She knew that she would never commit suicide; that was a discussion she'd had with herself a long time ago, when it seemed that she'd lost everything and there wasn't much left to live for. She'd reminded herself of a very simple maxim, which was that tomorrow was a new day, and the sun would most likely come out and shine.

"Bet your bottom dollar," she hummed, as she bustled her way into the kitchen at Carnance Books.

It occurred to her that DS Lander had been right, too. She'd said that, if the person who pushed that girl from the cliffs is local, then it wouldn't take them long to discover there'd been a witness to the crime, and want to try to silence them, somehow. Nothing so easy as creating the conditions of madness for a woman who already lived with plenty of demons to begin with.

And that made her very, very angry.

It wasn't a bad emotion, for once. This time, she welcomed the fire in her belly, reminding her that she was alive, and capable of fighting back. She would not be cowed by someone who would hide behind mental illness, or mock it to hide their own nefarious deeds.

That person was a coward.

DS Lander came into the shop at around lunchtime, wearing a smile.

"Sorry to disturb you at work," she said, when Gabrielle excused herself for five minutes to hear what she had to impart. "I thought you'd want to hear the good news."

Good news?

She wasn't sure that the finding of a body could ever be considered 'good' news, exactly…

"Have you found something?"

"No, nothing like that," Jane said. "It's about the girl you tried to visit, yesterday."

"Tamsyn Bray?"

"The very same. Well, I'm a woman of my word, and I looked into everything you'd told me. On the face of it, things did look pretty bad, with her friends asking about her, and whatnot. Anyway," she said, shaking her head, "after reading the posts and considering the message you'd sent her, plus the sudden lack of mobile phone, I was worried she'd been hurt, so I obtained a search order. We went in this morning to see what we might find, and the whole place was cleared out, already! No old food, or laundry hanging around the place. She must have come back herself, late last night or early this morning, to grab her stuff."

Jane paused to suck in a breath.

"Obviously, I asked around. That's when I learned that she'd met a man while she was at a festival, recently, and decided to move in with him in Cardiff."

"Cardiff?" Gabi repeated.

"Apparently so." Jane nodded. "Aren't you relieved? I know I am."

Gabi didn't think or feel anything, and then a sense of disappointment kicked in.

"I thought we'd found her," Gabi said, disconsolately. "I really thought we'd found the missing woman."

Jane sighed. "Gabi, isn't it *good* news that a girl you thought was missing and probably dead…isn't?"

"Of course," she replied, and told herself not to be macabre. "It's great news."

Why, then, did she feel dissatisfied?

CHAPTER 28

Jane couldn't stay, for she had other duties and her own family to attend to, and Gabrielle returned to her task of setting up a new counter display without much enthusiasm.

She should be happy that Tamsyn Bray had found a new man and was, probably this very moment, on the road to Cardiff.

So why did she feel something was missing?

Once the books were arranged in an attractive tower formation, she stuck a little cardboard sign on them that read, 'BOOK OF THE WEEK' and, as the shop was quiet, she left Zack in charge of the till and went back to her office for a few minutes to sit quietly and think.

It didn't take long for her to do what, she admitted to herself, she'd planned to do all along.

She brought up Facebook, and checked Tamsyn's page again.

This time, to her surprise, things looked different. In the first place, the privacy settings had been changed, so that she could no longer see the comments left by her friends or family, and her profile picture was greyed out.

But she could still read any private messages and, when she went into the inbox, it was to find a reply waiting:

Dear Ms Adams,

Thank you very much for your response to my application! Sorry you couldn't get me on the phone, but I managed to drop it down the loo and it hasn't worked since. I'll get a new one sorted soon.

Thanks for offering to keep me on file, but I'm actually moving to Wales now, and don't plan to return any time soon.

Have a great summer,

Tamsyn

Gabi re-read the message, which had been sent at 23:05 the previous evening, searching for clues as to the girl's mental state, or…something.

But there it was, in black and white.

As Jane had said, she should be pleased Tamsyn was still alive, and not torn apart by the waves.

And then, a little voice began to whisper in her mind.

If I'd killed a woman and didn't want people to find out, I'd keep an eye on her social media accounts and pretend she was still alive…

She had no proof that message had been written by Tamsyn, after all. Anyone could have logged in using the saved details on her laptop, and typed anything they wanted.

Gabrielle steepled her hands together and rested her chin on top, as she thought back. One of Tamsyn's friends had been called 'Ellie Dawn', she was sure of it.

A moment later, she was searching the name, and a short list of possible candidates came up. Scrolling through them, Gabi chose the one she seemed to recognise from her comment on Tamsyn's page, showing her posing by a beach—which seemed to be a theme amongst their circle—wearing an improbably short summer mini-dress and sporting purple dyed hair.

Clicking on the girl's face, a profile popped up on her screen monitor showing lots of images of Ellie with friends, including Tamsyn, and Gabi knew she'd found the right one. She found the 'message' button, and decided to meddle a little bit more.

"Knock, knock," came a deep voice.

She froze, her fingers snatching away from the keyboard, and looked around to find Luke lounging in the doorway, still dressed in his city gear of a well-fitting suit, shirt and tie. He'd even thrown a bit of gel in his hair and, despite her mind being occupied with other things, there was plenty of space for her to be able to commit the appealing image to memory.

"Well, don't you look smart," she said, and, before she could stop herself, she rose from the chair to wind her arms around his neck and give him a long, lingering kiss. "Welcome home."

"I'll have to go away more often," he said, with a broad grin. "How are you feeling, after what happened?"

"I—" She didn't feel the same as she used to, in the lovely little cottage Nell had given her. How could she?

"Because I've been doing some thinking, on the train home," Luke said, keeping his voice casual and light. "We've been spending so much time together anyway, it occurred to me that you might as well consider my home your home—even temporarily. That way, you don't have to worry about somebody entering your cottage and messing with your stuff, because I'd be there most of the time. Not to mention, the greatest guard dog in the world…Actually, scratch that—all it takes is a bit of meat and a well-placed tickle behind the ears to placate Madge."

He looked over his shoulder to where the dog was being spoiled by Nell, who had a bowl of ham off-cuts waiting for her.

Gabi grinned.

"There's no pressure," he added, a bit nervously. "It's just an offer."

This was a big deal for him, she realised suddenly. The house he lived in had been built for him and his wife, but Isobel had never lived in it, because she'd died before it was finished. That meant he'd lived there alone for the most part, aside from the company of his Labrador. He'd made the space uniquely his own, reflecting his own style and taste, and it would be hard to think of sharing it with anyone else, who might easily come in and disturb the balance.

It was a big step, even for a couple who had been in a relationship for a while, let alone a matter of weeks.

"Thank you," she said. "I'd love that. Why don't you come round later and help me pack up the wagon? I hope you have a spare dressing room for all my clothes."

This last remark was delivered with a poker-face, and, to his credit, he tried to mask his obvious dismay.

"How many clothes do you have, woman?"

She laughed. "Not as many as all that," she said. "I was only teasing. A couple of drawers would be wonderful."

"Now, that, I can manage."

While Luke took himself off to change out of his suit and get down to the serious business of painting, Gabi returned to her task, which was to type a message to Tamsyn's friend, Ellie:

Dear Ellie,

You don't know me, so I'm sorry to contact you out of the blue like this, but I wanted to ask about your friend Tamsyn to check whether she was all right. Have you heard from her? I tried contacting her last week, but had no reply until today, when she said she was going to be moving to Wales. I was concerned, because her mobile phone wasn't working, and I needed to contact her regarding a job application she made.

It would be great to hear from you!

Best wishes,
Gabrielle Adams

She clicked 'send' and then shut her computer down, determined not to think of it anymore. She'd done her civic duty—more than that, really—and, at the very least, she hoped her message would prompt Tamsyn's friend to check on her whereabouts more seriously, and to think beyond the faceless façade of a social media platform.

People were not who they said they were.

Didn't that apply in real life, too? the little voice inside her head asked.

Were the people around her who they said they were, or did they leave double lives?

You're a paranoid mess, Gabi.

Mark's words floated to the surface of her mind, and they hurt, but only for a moment. Then, she shoved them resolutely aside, determined never to doubt herself again.

Even if she had washed her hands three times that morning.

CHAPTER 29

"I want to take a closer look."

Luke's paintbrush paused mid-air, and he looked around the side of the easel.

"At the painting?" he asked. "It's not done, yet."

"No, at Gull's Point," Gabi said, twisting around in her chair to look out of the living room window and across to the western headland. "I've been avoiding it, I suppose, but now I want to have a look and see the terrain for myself. It's only seven o'clock; we could have a nice stroll with the dog before the sun goes down."

Luke stretched out his arms, and made a sound of agreement.

"You might want to put some clothes on, first," he said, with a wink. "Unless you want to scandalise the neighbours."

Gabi almost snorted.

"I don't think a single one of them could be scandalised," she said. "But you're probably right."

She reached for the robe that was draped nearby, and started to put it on.

"On second thought..." he said, walking towards her with a glint in his eye. "Let's not be too hasty."

A cool forty minutes later, they stepped out into the balmy July evening with Madge in tow, armed with small flasks of coffee and a packet of dog biscuits, in time to catch the sunset.

"Jane and Nell said there was a set of cliff stairs that nobody uses anymore," Gabi said. "Apparently, they're too dangerous?"

Luke nodded.

"Yes, the council designated them 'unsafe' and, generally, people don't use them."

"Generally?"

"Well..." He looked sheepish. "I've used them once or twice, in an emergency. Say, for example, when I've left something in the car, and I can't access the car park in the usual way. It's a longer walk, but if you don't mind heights, and I don't, then you can trot up the steps and walk east around the clifftop to the car park, or west to Gull's Point."

She was stricken.

"But—what if you fall—what if—"

"Gabi," he said, taking her hand in his. "I'm a grown man. I'm careful, I promise you. Besides, I'm hardly the only person who still uses those stairs—I've seen Jackson going back and forth a few times, when he's missed the tide. There's a good view of the steps, from that side of the garden," he explained, pointing to the edge of the lawn. "But, if it worries you so much, I won't use them anymore."

She nodded, and he gave her a lopsided smile, tugging her into the circle of his arms.

"Does this mean you care about my wellbeing, Gabrielle?"

"Maybe."

He lowered his head and kissed her deeply.

"I care about you, too," he said softly. "Let's agree that neither of us will take unnecessary risks. Okay?"

She nodded, and they began making their way down to the beach.

"Have there been any more incidents at the cottage?" he asked her, as they passed it by.

"I've hardly been back there to know," she replied. "But there was one other thing that happened today. When I came back from lunch with you, I found that someone had switched everything around on my desk. It's a small thing, but noticeable. I checked with Nell, but she hadn't been back there, at all—she'd been too busy serving customers, and it was apparently the same for Pat, Elena and Zack."

"They're persistent, whoever they are," Luke said, and she sensed the latent anger simmering beneath the surface. "Where are the access points, if somebody wanted to get into your office?"

"There's the swing door leading from the shop to the kitchen, and from there, a connecting door to the back office," she said. "There's a back door to the kitchen, too, which leads there."

She pointed towards the northern wall, at the back of the shop.

"There is a window in the office, which might feasibly be big enough for someone to squeeze through, but it would be an effort."

"It wouldn't take long," he argued. "If someone had a mind to, and knew the routines of the shop."

She nodded, feeling unsettled.

"What I can't fathom is, why hasn't a body turned up, yet?"

"It must have been the rip tide," he replied. "The current could take a body far, far out into deep water and it might be weeks before it turns up—if ever. It's a pity we don't know who she was."

Gabi cleared her throat.

"Actually, I think I might have found out," she replied. "Entirely by chance, but I have a strong feeling I know who she was, Luke."

And she told him the full story.

"Why didn't you mention this before?"

"I...I don't know. I suppose I wanted to be sure. It's hard, when at least half of the people around you believe you've got an overactive imagination."

"Have you had a reply from the girl—from Tamsyn's friend?"

"Not yet, but, since we were speaking of risk, I should probably admit that it was risky to send that message to Ellie Dawn," she said. "Somebody out there knows who I am, knows what I saw, and who I believe to be the victim. If they killed Tamsyn Bray, they might have access to her laptop or her mobile phone, which means they can probably find a way to check her social media accounts, e-mails and so on. They'd already know I'd messaged her, which is why they sent that bogus reply—"

"Allegedly," he put in, for balance.

"Allegedly," she agreed. "And if that's the case, when Tamsyn's other friend gets in touch to ask where she is, and maybe mentions that some woman called Gabrielle has been asking after her, they'll know I haven't given up—far from it. They'll know that I suspect the whole story, about her having cleared out of the caravan to move to Cardiff with some bloke she met, is complete rubbish."

He listened, nodding silently as they began to walk across the beach, which by now was deserted.

"So what's the next step? Speak to Jane again?"

"I've tried, but I think her patience with me is wearing thin. From her perspective, she's followed up everything she possibly can, and my pressuring her to do more comes off as pushy, especially without any real evidence to support it."

"There's nothing wrong with being pushy, if it's for a good cause. We can talk to her together, if you like."

She reached for his hand, and linked her fingers with his own.

"I'll wait to see whether I hear anything from Ellie, then I'll take it to the police."

By now, they'd reached the base of the western headland, which jutted out in the shape of a seagull's beak, hence the name 'Gull's Point'. The water concealed a long ridge of craggy rock, which could be deadly for passing boats, and there was a natural inlet which harboured the dangerous rip tide so many people had warned her about. At low tide, a network of caves was accessible by foot, leading into the bowels of the cliff, but, at high tide, the water rushed in, closing them off from the world.

Unexpectedly, Madge bounded ahead, making directly for one of the caves.

"Madge!" Luke called, and swore softly. "We'll be here all night, looking for her. She never usually runs on ahead like that. Madge!"

They picked up the pace and, upon reaching the shadowed entrance to one of the caves, Luke set his mobile phone to 'torch' mode.

"You don't have to come in, if you don't want to," he told her.

But Gabi was tired of living in fear, and wanted to know what lay inside the rock.

"I'll be okay," she said, and with a nod, he led the way inside.

There was a hollow eeriness to the caves that made Gabrielle shiver.

"Smugglers used this cave network to hide their wares from the excise men," Luke told her. "There's about a mile of cave tunnels, but they're like a spaghetti junction; they run into one another."

"Has anyone ever made a map?" she asked, hearing the echo of Madge's paws somewhere up ahead.

"Probably, but I've never seen one," Luke replied, shining the torch ahead of them so they wouldn't fall. There was a mix of sand and rock at their feet, with all manner of potholes designed to trip the unsuspecting visitor.

"How well do you know your way around?" she asked him.

"Pretty well, by now," he said. "But I wouldn't dare say that to Nell or Jackson. They like to think it's a secret only few can know."

Their voices reverberated off the darkened walls, and the scent of the sea was strong, clinging to the inside of their nostrils. Seaweed, lichen and all manner of other scents mingled and clung to the limestone, so it was both hard and slimy, which Gabrielle discovered when she braced a hand against one of the walls.

"Eugh—it's like gunge," she said, with a laugh.

"I forgot to say, try not to touch the walls," he said, blandly.

"Gee, thanks."

"Don't mention it," he said, and threw a smile over his shoulder which managed to look devilish in the thin white light of his torch.

"Madge!" he called out. "Madge, come!"

But there was no 'woof' and the accompanying stampede of footsteps they'd come to expect from her.

"Dumb dog," he muttered, affectionately. "She'll need a bath with all the trimmings, when we get back. That's after I disinfect her and everything she touches."

Gabi laughed, trying not to feel too claustrophobic in the dark tunnel.

"You already told me she's a diva," she said.

"She earns the title," he said. "Madge! Treats! Chicken treats!"

He rattled the bag he held in his hand, which was usually a sure way of attracting her attention, but there was no sign of her, and the snuffling sound they'd heard had since stopped.

"Luke, do you think she's okay?"

"To be honest, I'm starting to get a bit worried. We only have another fifteen, twenty minutes tops, before we really need to get out of here. If the tide comes in, it rises all the way to the top of the caves, so we'd be trapped if we stay too long."

"Which means Madge could be trapped, too?"

"Yes," he said, and picked up his pace, calling out to the dog more urgently than before.

But there was no sign of her, and fifteen minutes later, they'd walked in circles around the different tunnels. When they began to feel the sludge of water beneath their feet, Luke was forced to make an executive decision.

"Time to go," he said, and took her hand again.

"We can't leave her here," Gabi protested.

"What choice do we have?" He rounded on her, eyes filled with frustration. "You wanted to see the caves—well, now we've seen them. If we stay, there's a good chance we'll be drowned, or dragged out to sea, just like—"

He cut himself off, not wishing to upset her any further.

"You can say it," she said softly. "Just like that woman, and just like your wife."

He said nothing further, but focused all his attention on finding the correct route out of the caves before the tide swept in, never more conscious of what he'd been forced to leave behind.

CHAPTER 30

Luke was very quiet when they finally made it out of the caves, wading through sea water that was up to their knees already, and getting higher all the time. Once they were clear of it, and back onto the thin strip of sand left on the beach, he turned and scanned the water for any sign of the dog.

"She isn't there," he said softly.

"Luke," Gabi said, and pointed towards higher ground, almost at the top of Gull's Point. "Isn't that her?"

He raised his eyes to follow the direction of her finger, and his face broke into a smile again.

"Madge!"

The dog turned in circles, unsure of how to get down without trying to jump into the water, far below.

"Stay there!" He held both hands up, palms out in the universal gesture.

"How are we going to get her down?" Gabi asked.

"She'll have to try the cliff steps," he said. "Dogs are generally more sure-footed than humans, and it's either that or try to swim."

Gabi held a hand to her mouth, her eyes tracing the cliff steps to try to find the best route down.

"What's happening?"

They both turned to see Jackson approach, a cold beer in hand.

"Saw you both out here, and thought you looked like you needed some help. What's up?"

"It's Madge," Luke said. "She ran into the caves before I had a chance to put a lead on her, chasing some scent or another, and we couldn't get to her before the tide started coming in. We thought she was lost, but she's managed to wind up at the top of Gull's Point, and now she's stuck. I don't know how."

Jackson squinted up at the cliffside, and spotted the dog looking sorry for itself, whining and whimpering.

"Bummer," he said, with his usual flair for words. "Why don't you try and get her to use the steps? It was dry, today, so they won't be as slippery as usual. I'll stay here, in case she jumps into the water, if you guys head her off at the pathway."

Luke nodded, and put a grateful hand on the man's shoulder.

"Thanks, we'll head over there now."

It took time, but eventually Madge heard Luke's voice calling to her from the direction of the stairs and overcame her fear in order to take the first few steps. With plenty of encouraging cries of, 'TREATS!' and 'TICKLES!', she made it to the end, where she wasted no time in bounding up into Luke's arms like a small child.

Gabi watched them together and felt a lump rise to her throat.

She might only have been a dog, but Madge meant so much to the tall, quiet man she'd come to love, and Gabi couldn't bear it if he'd lost anything else to the sea.

Love?

Where had that word come from?

She watched them both for the next few minutes, saw the sloppy kisses and oily paws on his skin, and thought he was the gentlest man she'd ever met. For all his success, there was very little artifice about him, and he wasn't too proud to lie on the ground and let a dog roll all over him. She had a sudden vision of how he might be with small children, chasing them around the beach, splashing in the sea...

"Gabi?"

"Hmm?"

"I was asking whether you're ready?" Luke said, while the dog continued to nudge his leg.

"More than ready," she said.

They stopped briefly at Gabrielle's cottage to allow her to pick up some fresh clothes, and it became clear she'd had another visitor sometime during the day. This time, they'd taken the trouble to line up every sharp implement they could find in one long line on the kitchen counter, and had used one of the knives to attack the cushions in the living room, tearing a line through the nice, expensive-looking sofa Nell had recently purchased.

Gabrielle was devastated, and blamed herself.

"This is awful," she said, picking her way through the living room, where they'd really gone to town. "I'll replace everything."

"Nell will have insurance to cover this," Luke pointed out. "This wasn't your fault, Gabi. You locked the door, they entered unlawfully and caused criminal damage. As soon as we get home, we'll call the police and make a report."

"But first, Nell needs to see this."

He didn't argue, and went off to fetch her.

"The lousy, no-good, buggering bastards!" Nell declared, once she saw the extent of the damage. "Fancy, lining up weapons, as some sort of disgusting message. When we find out the name of this scumbag, they'll feel the rough end of my boot up their arse, and no mistake!"

"But the damage to your sofas, and curtains—"

"Pfft, never mind that," Nell said. "It's messy, and inconvenient, but they're replaceable and it isn't as if you won't have another sofa to sit on, while everything's being cleaned up. It's the knives I don't like. That's a mean, nasty thing to do, just like the empty pill box and the book."

"They're creative, at least," Luke muttered.

"I've called Jane—she says she'll come over with a constable first thing tomorrow to see the damage, take some prints and all that," Nell said. "This is the second time."

"The first time around, they wanted to convince me I'd taken the pills myself, and marked up the passages on suicide," Gabrielle said, feeling anger rise up in her belly. "They had a fair chance of convincing me, that time. But this? It makes no sense at all. I've never had any association with knives or sharp objects. It's sloppy, and perhaps gives away more about their mental state than mine."

They looked around at the angry slash marks, and at the knife left discarded on the floor with its tip now blunt from the abuse.

"They're frustrated," Luke agreed. "Angry that you've thwarted them, and, by the looks of things, that anger is escalating. We need to be careful, Gabi."

"It's like they had a tantrum, isn't it?" Nell muttered, and didn't notice the other two exchange a telling glance. "You didn't pack up and leave the first time, so now they're getting really insistent."

"It feels like a final warning," Gabi agreed, and thought of the e-mail she'd sent earlier that day to Ellie Dawn, before she'd known the extent of the damage.

"I'll ask Jude to patrol the house," Nell said. "He can keep watch for whoever comes and goes. I'm sorry, Gabi, I should have asked him to do that before now. I suppose I hoped—we all hoped—the last time was a one-off."

Gabrielle nodded. "That was my hope, too," she said. "I guess we were both wrong."

She knew then that it would never stop. It wouldn't stop until the perpetrator was caught, or she was gone. They'd given her an opportunity to leave; to pack her things and slink back to London with her tail between her legs, but she hadn't. This was her final chance, before there would be nowhere to run to.

But she was tired of running, especially from herself.

It was time to stick around and fight.

CHAPTER 31

When they returned to Luke's house, Gabrielle found there was a message waiting for her, on Facebook:

Hi Gabrielle,

Thanks for the message. I've been REALLY worried about Tam, as well. She hasn't replied to any of my messages for a while now, and I keep getting 'number unavailable' when I try to call. She replied to my message on her profile saying she was fine and that she'd be in touch, but it feels really weird. I sent her another message on here, and she wrote back today to say that she's moving to Cardiff, which is COMPLETELY out of the blue. I don't even know this guy she's supposed to have met, and she's still not over the guy from

Falmouth, so there's no way she would have gotten with anyone else so soon. That's what I think, anyway.

I've tried to contact her mum and dad, but they're not close and I don't think they've been in touch since she left home, so they're not interested. Please let me know if you hear from her, or else I think I should call the police.

Ellie x

Gabrielle was still digesting the content of that message, when there came the 'ping' of a notification to say that another message had been received.

Hurriedly, she clicked to open it, and saw that the sender was Tamsyn.

Hi again,

I'm sorry to contact you again, but I wasn't sure who else I could trust, and you seemed so nice.

A lot of people have been trying to contact me, but something has happened, and I can't tell them about it. I do need help, and I was wondering if you could meet me? I couldn't stay at the caravan site anymore, because I knew he'd find me there. I can't come into Carnance because he'd see me, for sure. Please can you meet me? Maybe at Gull's Point, and I can explain what happened. I don't want anyone to see me, so night-time would be better. Ten-thirty tomorrow night? After that, I'll be leaving for good.

Anyway, I understand if you don't want to, I'm putting you to a lot of trouble. Thank you for listening, and for caring about what happens to me.

Tam x

P.S. Please don't tell anyone—especially the painter. You can't trust him. Look at his paintings and you'll find one of me.

Gabrielle read the last line three times, and each time it said the same thing.

The painter...you can't trust him...he has a painting of me...

There was no mistake.

But why would Luke have a painting of Tamsyn Bray, unless he'd known her? And, if he had, why hadn't he mentioned it before now?

Because he had something to hide.

"Any news?" Luke asked, coming to look over her shoulder.

She set the laptop aside, closing it before he had time to read the messages.

"Just one from Ellie, saying she's been worried, too," Gabi said. "She's going to try to contact Tamsyn's parents."

Luke nodded, then looked at her closely.

"Are you all right?" he asked. "You seem…strange."

She forced a laugh.

"Flattery will get you everywhere," she said, and came to her feet. "I was just thinking, I need something to distract me from all the talk of murder. Hey! You haven't shown me all your paintings yet, and you *did* say I could choose one, in exchange for sitting for you."

He was happy enough to oblige.

"It's a bit late, so the light won't be as good, but… okay. Come with me."

He led her upstairs and along a corridor to a part of the house she hadn't seen before: the attic. They took a narrow, spiral staircase and emerged into a fully renovated space, all painted in white, with banks of skylights on each side to allow for maximum light. It spanned the whole length of the house, and there were dozens and dozens of canvases of differing shapes and sizes stacked against the walls and on purpose-built shelves. There was another enormous shelving unit where Luke stored his materials, an architect's table and tall chair for detailed work, a long sofa and a small kitchenette—and that was just at a glance.

"You don't do things by halves, do you?"

"I try not to," he agreed, noting the odd tone to her voice once again, and unable to pinpoint its cause. "What would you like to see, first? There are some that are earmarked for gallery exhibitions, but the others are open season, for you."

"Um, let's see. How about portraits? Have you done many of those?"

"A few," he said, and considered where they might be. "Let's start over here."

He led her to a stack of paintings and began turning them around, so she could see each one in turn. Despite her misgivings following the message she'd just received, Gabi couldn't help but admire his skill in capturing the shape and form of each person—and they were all different, ranging in age, skin colour, size and setting.

But none of them was Tamsyn Bray.

"They're all lovely," she said, and began to feel the tension leave her shoulders.

"Thank you," he said. "Those were all completed about two years ago, and hung in the Padstow gallery for a while. Some were sold, but these ones I wanted to keep. There are some more portraits over here."

He led her to a second stack, and this time he paused before showing her the first.

"I hope you're not easily offended," he said. "This is the nude selection."

He said it with such an air of naughtiness, she couldn't help but smile.

"I'm sure my constitution can take it," she assured him.

He flipped the canvases one by one, talking through each one as a clinical subject, discussing shape and form, the line of the brow or the way the light fell this way or that, until he came to one of a young woman with long, dark hair, with her back turned to him and her face in profile.

Gabrielle searched the woman's face, trying to decide if that was Tamsyn Bray.

"Who was this model?" she asked.

"Hmm," he said, and looked on the back of the canvas to see if he'd made a note. "This one was painted last year, as part of a nude series for the Tate St Ives. I'm afraid I can't remember her name, but I could always check my invoices. Each life model is paid for their time, unless they happen to be the artist's girlfriend, in which case she gets to take home a painting…"

He slid an arm around her shoulders, and didn't seem to notice that the tension had returned.

"Why do you ask? It's perfectly normal, you know, to use life models," he added, thinking that she might have been uncomfortable on that score. "It doesn't mean anything to me; it's like a doctor looking at a patient."

"I don't mind that."

"Phew! They're not all young twenty-somethings," he assured her. "I've had life models in their seventies and eighties, of all sexes."

She looked at the faces he showed her, and thought again of how much he saw of these people; how well he had captured their spirit, if there was such a thing.

"Well? Do you have a favourite?" he asked.

"Not at the moment," she said, feeling tired all of a sudden. "I'll have to think about it—there's too much choice."

"Take your time," he said. "Or tell me if you have a favourite view, and I'll paint it for you."

Had anyone ever said anything so romantic? Gabrielle wondered. And yet, her happiness was now tainted by a small, poisonous thread of doubt. There was still every chance that 'Tamsyn' was not Tamsyn at all, and was, in fact, her killer, hoping to lure her away.

Then again, it might be a young girl in need of help.

She already knew what she would do.

CHAPTER 32

The following morning dawned misty and grey, but the weather did little to mar the ethereal beauty of the cove, which ascended from the fog that rolled in waves off the water to curl through its houses and pathways like ghostly fingers. Gabrielle watched it from the bedroom window of her cottage, while DS Lander and one of her constables moved through the rooms of the house, taking notes and photographs of the damage. She heard them talking to Nell and Luke, taking their statements about what they'd seen, while her eyes strayed up towards Gull's Point, on the far western headland.

She hoped she'd made the right judgment call, but she'd know before the day was out.

"She seems subdued," Jane remarked, as she and Nell seated themselves at a corner table at the bookshop with a couple of hot croissants, later that morning. "Then again, she's been through a lot."

Nell heaved a long sigh. "She's been through the wringer," she agreed. "It's no wonder her nerves are shot."

Jane glanced across the room, to where Gabi and Luke appeared to be engaged in a heated argument. "Uh-oh," she said. "Trouble in paradise?"

"They had some sort of lovers' tiff, last night, as far as I can tell," Nell said, conspiratorially. "Something about Luke having done a nude painting of a woman."

"Isn't that his job?" Jane said, accepting the cup of filter coffee Nell offered her.

"You'd have thought," Nell agreed, shaking her head at the younger generation. "Apparently, it was to do with it being a *particular* woman—I've no idea who, but it's caused an enormous bust-up."

Jane tutted. "That's a shame. They seemed so well matched."

"Perhaps they'll manage to work it out," Nell said, and waved to Jackson, who wandered into the shop, eyed up the warring couple, and then helped himself to a pastry. "Then again, perhaps not. She's got a stubborn streak, that one."

Nell took a sip of coffee. "There's all that business about the woman on Facebook, too."

"What do you mean?"

"Luke seems to think Gabi has become obsessed with finding some woman she saw on Facebook—somebody she happened to reject for the staff position here, apparently. She's got it into her head that this woman's the one she saw being pushed off the cliff."

Jane knew the one she meant, but kept her own counsel.

"Then, there's that empty pill bottle..." Nell shook her head, sadly. "It might have been an intruder but, on the other hand...she's troubled, that one. We've all been humouring her, but there's only so much you can do."

"I saw Luke and Gabi having an argument outside," Jackson said, coming to join them at the table. "What's all that about?"

"She's asked for the morning off, so she can move her things back out of his place and into her own," Nell told him. "It's not looking good."

"Is that so? I could always head over to the cottage, this evening, to console her—make sure she doesn't feel lonely."

Jane laughed.

"Don't you dare," Nell warned him. "That girl needs peace and quiet, and you're neither of those things. Leave her alone tonight—I'll be making sure everyone else does."

"Spoilsport," Jackson muttered. "But don't worry, I'll give it a day or so, before I offer her my shoulder to cry on."

"He's incorrigible," Nell said, and talk moved on to other things.

The remainder of the day passed at a glacial pace, with Gabrielle going through the motions of serving customers, stacking shelves, discussing current reads, clearing plates and balancing books, until she was about ready to explode. When the evening finally came around, she was emotionally drained, having been wired with an excess of adrenaline that kept her going, but now left her feeling exhausted.

And it wasn't over yet.

She watched the last of the holidaymakers pack up and depart until the cove was silent once more, its waters still, as though the sea itself was watching and waiting to see what would happen next.

Gabi settled down to wait.

Shortly before ten-thirty, the lone figure of Detective Sergeant Jane Lander walked along the top of the headland towards Gull's Point, dressed in a long coat and jeans, with the hood pulled up around her face. The water crashed against the rocks far below, as it had done the other time, and the wind pushed her onward, not as strongly as it had before, but with the same urgency.

Reaching the pinnacle, she saw she was the first to arrive, and checked the time again on the watch at her wrist.

Ten thirty-five.

Gabrielle Adams was not the kind of woman to be late for anything, if she could help it, which was a source of alarm.

Was she going to come?

The message Jane sent to Gabi had been drafted and re-drafted numerous times, until she found just the right tone; just enough neediness to appeal to a character like her, who welcomed the opportunity to try to help birds that were even more wounded than herself.

Pathetic.

There was nothing more irritating, more sycophantic, than a do-gooder.

When another five minutes passed without any sign of Gabrielle, she could feel the anger begin to rise; the same anger that had led Jane to Gull's Point that first time, and had brought her there again.

Selfish, entitled, smug little bitch.

What did Gabi know about any of it? Nothing. She knew nothing, and yet she'd taken a wrecking ball to their lives simply by *existing*, by seeing something she should never have seen, and then opening her big mouth to anyone who would listen.

It should have been easy, getting rid of someone like Gabrielle.

Wasn't she the sorry little woman from London, who'd suffered such a traumatic ordeal?

What did Gabi really know about trauma?

She could tell her a thing or two, about how lives could be turned upside down. She could tell her about having to put on a brave face, each and every day, pretending to the world that nothing had happened, when, all the while, she'd wanted to take that woman's head between her hands and just…crush it.

Jane was breathing hard now, and the anger was like a roar inside her head.

She had not come this far, and sacrificed so much, to lose it all now.

Not for Gabrielle Adams, and not for Tamsyn Bray.

CHAPTER 33

The view from Gull's Point really was superlative.

It was possible to see for miles around, during the daytime, whilst at night...

At night, Jane could see everything.

She could see Pat and Jude Barker brushing their teeth in their bathroom, before shuffling through to their bedroom, pulling back the chintzy bedspread and turning off the lights to sleep

Nell Trelawney and her wastrel of a son were next.

Through the long, glass windows of their fancy conservatory, she could see them moving around in the kitchen, stacking the dishwasher to run overnight, turning off the television and, soon after, the lights.

Then, Luke Malone. The bogtrotter from Dublin, who everyone seemed to love.

Lucky him.

What she wouldn't give to be truly loved; to be able to trust in it, build a life on it, and a family...

She brushed away sudden tears, angrily.

Instead, she had to settle for lies, and pretend they were true.

She could see Luke moving around the enormous house he'd built for himself, naked from the waist up, brushing his teeth while he went around each room, turning off the lights.

Good.

That only left Gabrielle.

Clever little Gabrielle Adams, who just wouldn't take the hint.

The lights in her windows continued to burn until almost eleven, until, finally, they were extinguished, and all was quiet and dark in Carnance Cove.

That's right, she thought. *Go to sleep. It'll be easier, that way.*

It seemed Nell had been right about Gabi and her boyfriend having had a fight. She was alone in the cottage, and that was just perfect.

When Jane could be sure that nothing stirred below, she began the long descent, picking her way down the cliff steps leading from Gull's Point to Carnance. It wasn't ideal, but she had a job to do, and she would do it by any means necessary.

The steps were mossy and worn, covered with bird excrement and other things, but it was the only way down to the cove and this was the last chance she would have to finish the job.

Gabi wouldn't stop digging.

If only she'd stopped digging.

It was a heady walk, exposed as she was to the worst of the wind coming in from the east, buffeting her against the cliff wall, only to whip around and begin all over again. It was fortunate, too, that Jane was of strong constitution, because the height and the gradient of the rocky stairway was dizzying. She felt her way down through the darkness, too cautious to turn on a torch. The risk of death was great, but the risk of exposure was even greater, and it was not one she was prepared to take.

Jane made her way directly to the back door of Gabrielle's cottage, just as she'd done both times before. Moving on silent footsteps through the shadows, she was little more than a whisper of movement in the night as she slipped around the back of the short row of houses, making directly for the one at the end. She found it locked, just as expected, with a chair propped up against the back of the handle, which was also just as expected.

She pulled on a pair of nitrile gloves, then retrieved a length of shaven bamboo from beneath the hedgerow, where she'd left it the last time. She slipped it beneath the door and used it to lever the chair legs up and further along—just enough to allow her to unlock the door and catch the chair before it fell.

The door opened with barely a creak, and closed just as softly behind her.

She stood perfectly still, listening, checked the length of rope in her pocket, and then moved quickly towards the staircase. Her tread was careful and quiet, cushioned by the thick-pile carpet on the runner, until she reached the landing, where she stood very still once more, listening intently.

She opened the bedroom door, and stepped inside.

Through the darkness, she saw the outline of Gabrielle sleeping. She heard the rhythmic rise and fall of her chest and even that simple, everyday motion was enough to bring forth a haze of anger.

How *dare* she carry on as if nothing had happened, as if the world hadn't changed, irreversibly?

How *dare* she potter about, reading and chatting away to the people of Jane's home county, as if she'd known them all their lives and knew what made them tick?

She knew nothing.

Nothing!

So her fiancé had broken it off, back in London. Boo hoo! She'd moved somewhere else and, *abracadabra*, she meets someone new, someone who actually seemed not to mind the fact she's a walking wreck, with her hand-washing and her re-arranging and her sad little panic attacks.

It made her sick.

Jane Lander felt hate course through her body, revelled in it, rejoiced in it, for it would help her to do what needed to be done.

Did anybody think she *wanted* this to happen?

She hadn't wanted any of it to happen. Not the first morning, when that girl…that little *trollop* had wandered over to her while she'd pushed Hattie on the swings at the play park, and calmly told her that Pete was in love with her, was planning to leave his family to be with her, and it was high time everyone got used to the idea.

She hadn't wanted to believe it.

She'd laughed at the girl—for that's all she was really, at twenty-two. Nothing more than a little dreamer, with a crush on her husband.

She'd told her so, roundly, and sent her on her way.

But the seed had been planted, and she needed to know for sure. That's when she'd started checking his phone messages, and his bank accounts.

But it hadn't been either of those.

It was his university e-mail account; the one he was supposed to use to discuss all his lofty notions about marine life, not to send filthy e-mails to a girl half his age, telling her all about what he planned to do with her, the next time he could get away from his wife.

His wife.

The woman he'd professed to love, whom he'd married eleven years ago and who had borne him two beautiful children, one of whom was less than a year old.

All of that, thrown on the scrap heap.

The girl had been eager to meet, in the end. Only too *eager* to brag about the things she'd done, telling her detail upon disgusting, stomach-churning detail of how, when and where, uncaring of the destruction she'd caused.

She hadn't intended to push her.

Truly, she hadn't.

She just wouldn't stop talking.

She kept on, and on, and on, until the sound had become a buzz in her ears, growing louder and louder until it drowned out even the noise of the storm; until she could stand it no more.

Then, a blessed silence, and all her troubles extinguished.

Or so it would have been, were it not for the woman who lay sleeping in front of her.

Jane reached into the pocket of her coat and pulled out a length of rope, which she wound between both fists.

Later, she'd make it look like a suicide.

Eyes burning, chest pounding, Detective Sergeant Jane Lander made her way across the room, her step light and her mind set on one outcome, and one alone.

She peeled back the covers just as the lights blazed on, and she spun around, her face a comical mask of surprise.

"It's over, Jane."

Luke stood in the doorway, fully dressed, his eyes flat and hard.

"Put the rope down, now, and move away from the bed."

"She'd never have come close," the sleeping figure said, and Jane turned to find that it was Nell, and not Gabrielle, climbing from the bed.

She spun around to the window, where she could see Jackson standing guard beneath.

"Jude is at the back door," Nell told her. "Everyone is here, Jane. Everyone knows it was you who killed that girl."

"It—this isn't what it seems," she said, thinking fast. "I came—to—to check on Gabrielle, after all that's happened."

"After all *you've* done," Luke corrected her, and turned to call over his shoulder. "Constable!"

When her junior officer stepped forward and began to make the arrest, Jane's face twisted into something grotesque.

"You think you're all so bloody smart, don't you?" she snarled. "You think you wouldn't do the same, given the choice? Women like Tamsyn Bray, and Gabrielle Adams, are all the same. They're sent to destroy. Remember that!"

The constable grasped her arm with a none-too-gentle hand, pinned it behind her back and slapped a pair of handcuffs on her wrists.

"I am arresting you on suspicion of the murder of Tamsyn Bray, and of the attempted murder of

Nell Trelawney," he said. "You do not have to say anything, but anything you do say—"

Her snarling cries turned into great, wracking sobs as she looked around the room, at the faces of people she'd once counted as friends but who now looked upon her as a stranger.

"Why, Jane? Why did you do it?"

She turned to look at Nell, and through the blur of tears, she replied, "Because she was going to take it all away from me, Nell. I couldn't let that happen."

With that, she turned back, and allowed herself to be led away.

Madge let out a warning bark at the door, which became a happy one when she recognised the tall figure making his way across the dark lawn.

"Who is it, girl?" Gabi whispered, from the dark interior of Luke's living room.

"It's only me," Luke said, and tapped on the window pane.

Gabrielle rushed forward to unlock the door.

"Well?" she asked, anxiously. "What happened?"

Luke reached across to turn on a light, then simply crossed the room in a couple of strides and enveloped her in his arms, just to hold her and take some of the strain of the day from her shoulders onto his own.

"You were absolutely right," he said, and rubbed his cheek against the top of her head. "It was Jane Lander."

Gabi closed her eyes, feeling both a sense of relief and one of devastation—mostly, for the woman's children, who would now be parted from their mother.

"Why did she do it?" she asked. "Did she tell you why?"

"Nell asked her, and she replied that Tamsyn was going to take everything from her," Luke said. "I imagine we'll find that she was one of Pete's students, at the University of Falmouth."

"I told you that Mark was having an affair with someone," she said. "When I found out, I felt betrayed and hurt, but never once did I imagine killing anyone for it, even if I had known the other woman's name."

"That's because you're not crazy," he said, with his usual candour. "It helps."

Gabrielle started to laugh, and looked up at him.

"Your plan worked," she said.

"She needed you alone," he said. "We created the conditions to make her believe that would be the case."

"I can't believe everybody came out to help," she said, with a touch of wonder.

"Why not? We protect our own, and you're one of us, now, Gabi."

She tried to remember a time when she'd ever really *belonged*, and found that she couldn't.

"Does this mean I get to use words like, 'dreckly'?"

"Let's not get ahead of ourselves."

CHAPTER 34

Six weeks later

Carnance Books & Gifts was a picture that night, if she did say so herself.

Gabrielle stood back to survey her handiwork from the terrace, taking in the new conservatory on its eastern wall, which would be hosting much of the evening's event, and the strings of lanterns lighting up the September evening, inviting people to step outside and enjoy a drink from the Books & Bevvies cart Jackson had helped to renovate, overlooking the sea. Inside, the shop floor had seen a minor transformation, and was now a sea of colour and texture, with row upon row of beautiful books facing customers like miniature works of art they could not only look at, but take home and read. Comfortable tables and chairs had been set up at regular intervals so that people could enjoy one of Pat's cakes or scones, while the Kids Corner now occupied a whole section of the shop floor, complete with play tent and optional dressing-up rail.

And that was only the beginning, Gabrielle thought.

Next year, once they'd all recovered, she'd talk about opening a second shop at nearby Lizard Point…

"You've worked wonders," Nell said, making her way out onto the terrace. "Everything looks wonderful, and most of the guests have arrived. That whatsherface, Saffron Furrows—"

"Wallows," Gabrielle said.

"—well, she's certainly wallowing in her public, tonight, that's for sure," Nell said, and laughed like a foghorn. "Never known anyone like the sound of their own voice, so much."

"She's become used to a lot of people telling her how wonderful and talented she is," Gabi explained. "It's gone to her head a bit, I'm afraid."

Nell harrumphed.

"She should come and stay with me for a couple of days," she said. "I'll soon knock that out of her."

Gabi laughed, thinking that she probably would achieve more in a couple of days than most people would in a couple of years.

"Anyway, I've come to remind you, she'll be starting her reading in ten minutes," Nell said.

"I'm coming now."

It was a motley crowd gathered at Carnance Books that evening.

There was the usual gang, including Nell, Jackson, Jude and Pat but, much to Gabi's chagrin, Luke had left a message to say he'd been delayed on the A30, the main road which ran like an artery through much of Western Cornwall connecting one major town to the next, but he'd be there as quickly as he could.

Aside from that, there was a full complement of booksellers, local press and book club aficionados, plus a good number of their regular customers and readers, who had come to enjoy a rare evening celebrating the re-birth of their beloved bookshop.

Aside from the star attraction, other authors had turned out, including those based locally and a man who needed no introduction—especially in his own mind.

"Gabrielle! Long time, no see."

Geoffrey Bowman leaned in to kiss her on both cheeks, and the first thing she noticed was that he'd finally decided to let his hair turn grey, which was a vast improvement.

Aside from that, he remained largely unchanged.

"You're looking as lovely as ever," he said, running his eyes over her in a manner she'd always found vaguely repulsive. "Look, when you've got a minute, I wanted to ask if you had any sway with that new bird—the one who took over your stable, after you left? Frannie something-or-other."

"Francesca Ogilvie," Gabrielle corrected him.

She'd invited her old friend, but received no reply, so she'd assumed that she hadn't been able to make it.

"That's the filly," he said, taking a healthy gulp of his wine. "Now, look, I need you to set her straight about a few things—"

To Gabrielle's surprise, Frenchie stepped into the shop at that precise moment, and her face blossomed into a smile...

Only to fade when she caught sight of the man she'd brought with her.

"Mark?"

"What?" Bowman asked, and turned around to see what had captured her attention. "Well, that's handy, isn't it? You can—"

"Excuse me, Geoff."

Gabrielle moved away, making directly for the two newcomers, who were already chatting to Nell like old friends. "This is a surprise," she said, and was proud of how level her voice sounded.

"There you are! Gabi, this is Francesca—"

"I know Frenchie and Mark very well," Gabi interrupted, taking in the way her friend's arm was linked with Mark's, and the way his hand curled around hers, possessively.

How did I miss that?

So blind...

"Frenchie was my best friend in London, and also happens to be Saffron's commissioning editor at Frenchman Saunders," Gabi said quietly, and the past tense was not lost on any of them. "Mark was my fiancé, and also happens to be Saffron's literary agent."

Nell's eyes widened, and her mouth pursed.

"Well, it's all very cosy in London, isn't it?" she said. "I'll leave you all to—ah—catch up."

She leaned in to speak to Gabi, as she left. "I'll be right over there, if you need me," she said, and put a supportive hand on her friend's arm.

Gabi looked between the pair of them. "I think congratulations are in order?"

"I've asked Frenchie to marry me," Mark said, with a tilt of his chin which, she happened to note, was considerably weaker than she'd previously recognised.

"I'm so sorry, Gabi," her friend whispered. "Neither of us meant for this to happen..."

Gabrielle held up her hands, and gave them both a broad smile.

"Please, let's not have any post-mortems. We all have new lives, now, and have met new people."

"Are you here with anyone?" Mark made a show of looking around.

"I'm here with a village full of excellent friends, a town full of wonderful customers, and the respect of my peers," she said. "As for the rest, that's no longer your concern."

She turned to her old friend, wondering how she could have been so misguided in her understanding of what constituted 'friendship' and offered her the best piece of advice she could think of.

"Enjoy the party," she said.

She nodded to them both, and stepped away.

Saffron's reading was a success, in that she was both an experienced orator and an engaging guest speaker, only too happy to spend plenty of time answering questions from the crowd. The content of her reading consisted of an excerpt from her latest book, *Girl, Not a Woman*, and it happened to contain another phrase Gabi seemed to recognise, even though she could not have heard it in that context before. She must have frowned, because Saffron caught her expression and was surprised enough to stutter, losing the thread of her reading for a short time before she picked it up again.

Aside from that, it was a great success.

"Gabrielle?" Saffron caught up with her, once the reading was over and she'd finished signing a long line of books.

Gabi smiled. "Thank you so much again for coming," she said, with just the right touch of deference she knew would appeal to a woman like Saffron. "I know everybody has loved having you here, today."

"Yes, quite," the other said, without a shred of modesty. "I couldn't help but notice, you seemed to pull a face at something I said—may I ask what offended you so much? I'm not accustomed to—"

"I'm sorry about that," Gabi said. "I thought I recognised one of the phrases you used, and I was trying to remember where I'd heard or read it before, that's all."

Saffron looked as though she was about to say something further, then they were interrupted.

"We'll talk later," she said.

Gabi smiled, and continued to mingle.

CHAPTER 35

Luke heaved a sigh of extreme frustration.

He'd been stuck in stationary traffic outside of Truro for over an hour, thanks to a heavy goods lorry having collided with a campervan, necessitating air ambulances, fire services and every other kind of flashing light that was available.

He thought of Gabi's party and felt terrible, knowing how much she'd been looking forward to it, and how much work had gone into the preparation.

"Nice one, Luke," he admonished himself, and reached across to change the station on the car radio. There were only so many 'smooth classics' that one man could stomach.

Thiiiis is Pirate FM, bringing you the latest from our news desk...

He listened with half an ear as they warned him to avoid the A30, which was heavily backed up owing to an overturned lorry, and yawned as they detailed the latest celebrity gossip. He was about to change the channel again, this time in protest, when something stopped him.

The infamous 'Tube Killer of London' attended the Old Bailey for a plea hearing today, where only three of four cases were brought against the man police have identified as Richard Slater, of Wood Green, East London. The Crown Prosecution Service has dropped its case against Slater in respect of one victim, Gabrielle Adams, a former publishing executive. The Metropolitan Police has declined to comment...

Luke listened in disbelief, certain Gabi had no idea about this development, otherwise she would have told him. On one level, he was pleased that she hadn't heard the news: this would come as a disappointing blow, not to mention a potential trigger to some of the old anxiety disorders, and she deserved to have at least one night where she would not be troubled with any of it.

Then another, much more potent, thought struck him.

If Richard Slater was not being charged with attempted murder, did that mean somebody else had been responsible for pushing her onto the tracks, that day?

If so—who?

He tapped a finger against the steering wheel, trying to think of any way to speed up the journey back to Carnance, but there was none—unless the car could sprout wings and fly.

The party was still in full swing when Gabrielle felt her mobile phone buzz, signalling a voicemail message had been received. It was such a rare occurrence, she excused herself from a particularly intense debate concerning Dostoyevsky versus Tolstoy, and went in search of a quiet corner where she could listen to it.

Her office proved to be such a place, and she sank onto her desk chair, wriggled her toes out of the heels she wore, and pressed the phone to her ear.

Hello, Miss Adams, this is PC Jepson calling from the Met Liaison Unit. I've been trying to call you, today, but haven't had any luck. If you could please return my call…

There was a beep, and the next message followed, left an hour after the first.

Hello, Miss Adams, this is PC Jepson calling you again… the time is, sixteen-oh-eight. I've tried calling you several times today, but without success. I'm sorry to let you know there's been a setback in your case against Richard Slater and the CPS have made the decision not to take forward their prosecution in respect of your attack of 18th December. If you could please call me back, I'll go through all the details with you…

Gabrielle thought she had misheard, and replayed the message, only to find it was exactly as she'd feared.

They'd dropped her case.

Why?

She brought up her e-mails, hoping to find something that might provide an explanation, and, sure enough, there were two e-mails from PC Jepson waiting for her.

She opened the first, and her eyes gobbled up the words, desperate to understand what could have gone so wrong. One paragraph stood out from the rest:

Following extensive CCTV analysis, we have been forced to conclude that the perpetrator detailed in the footage of your attack at South Kensington underground station on 18th December of last year was not the same as those in three other similar attacks. We understand this may come as a shock, and we offer our apologies for any inconvenience caused. Our investigation will continue…

"Inconvenience," she muttered, and could have laughed. They'd snatched away the only feeling of justice she'd been clinging to, and called it 'inconvenient'.

But the next logical question remained: if not Richard Slater, then who pushed her onto the tracks that night—and why?

Shivering, but not from cold, she clicked to open the next e-mail from PC Jepson. This one contained a video attachment, which she was unable to download thanks to the patchy Wi-Fi signal, and she could have screamed.

Please find attached video footage from 18th December, showing enhanced imagery of the unknown perpetrator. Please study this footage and let us know immediately if you recognise this person, or have any information to assist...

Gabi tried again to download the video, but since the internet in that part of the cove had all the power of a hamster running on a wheel, there was no chance of viewing it. The only place she would be able to download the video easily was at Luke's house, which she'd come to call 'home'.

Outside her office, the party was still swinging but not for much longer, since the tide was due to roll in within the hour. She should, by rights, stay to help Nell with the farewell fanfare, especially in respect of their VIP guest, but the need to see the face of the person who had pushed her that day was much greater and, if she hurried, she could be back within ten or fifteen minutes.

Her mind made up, Gabrielle pushed her shoes back on and made for the exit, slipping out into the twilight to hurry up the pathway to Luke's place.

She had no idea that somebody had witnessed her flight, nor that it was the same person whose face she was so eager to see.

Gabi gave the dog's head a brief scratch as she let herself into the house, then hurried towards the kitchen, where she'd left her laptop plugged in to charge the battery. She made a grab for it and brought up PC Jepson's email once more, pleased to see that, this time, when she clicked to open the attachment, it began downloading immediately.

It was a large file and would take a couple of minutes to appear, so she used the time to run a quick search for something else that had been bothering her all night.

The phrase Saffron had used, during her reading.

She could have sworn she'd heard it before, and that was the second time she'd experienced a sense of déjà-vu in respect of Saffron's latest work.

She typed into a search engine, "*I used to believe myself better than any, but I learned my journey was just one of many*" but received only PR pieces praising Saffron's book, which told her nothing new. Not expecting to find anything, she typed the phrase into the search bar on her laptop, instead, and a single file appeared in the results—one that had been sent to the 'trash' folder several months ago, and which she was only just able to retrieve. It was a manuscript entitled, *A Woman's Journey* and had been written by an author called Kelly Smith.

She didn't recognise the name, which was not unexpected, considering the volume of manuscripts which had once passed her desk, and the author's name was not artificial in any way. The date on the manuscript file was four years ago, but it had last been opened only a month before her fall.

Gabrielle had no memory of it, nor of the author, except perhaps a very weak feeling of recognition, but it was enough to prompt her to run a search of the author's name. She found no references to any published works, but she did find an obituary:

In loving memory of Kelly Ann Smith, wife of Andrew and mother of Charlie and George. Forever missed, and forever in our hearts. Gone but not forgotten.

With a sick sense of foreboding, Gabi opened the manuscript and scanned the first chapter, then the last, which was all she needed before drawing the obvious conclusion.

Saffron Wallows had plagiarised this woman's work.

The memories came flooding back so quickly she began to feel sick.

Discovering the old manuscript at Frenchman Saunders, and realising it had been plagiarised. Knowing that she'd been unwittingly complicit in publishing Saffron's work, in building her name and her brand, on a house of sand, and that it could cost them both dearly in terms of loss of reputation and livelihood. Arguing with Mark about her decision to reveal the truth, knowing Saffron was his best client and the scandal would hurt his career...She remembered it all.

So many people with a reason to silence her.

She opened the video file sent by the Met, and watched as the images began to roll.

She saw herself flying down the elevator, then hiding against the wall as she waited for the next train. She saw herself step forward as the train approached, and a lingering trail of passengers leaving as the train arrived on the opposite platform.

There!

She saw a single figure push through the flow of people from the opposite platform, walk swiftly towards her—and push. Air lodged in her throat as she remembered the sensation of falling, and she put a hand to her throat, unable to breathe, until she told herself it was all over.

It was in the past...

She could not make out a face, even with the images enhanced. The person had worn a hat, and a long, winter coat which was plain black and might have belonged to any number of people.

Closing the laptop, Gabi rested her head in her hands, and stayed there for longer than she intended, hardly aware that the sun had set, or that their guests had already begun to depart.

Then, the dog began to bark.

CHAPTER 36

Gabrielle's first thought was that Luke had finally come home, and she rose halfway from her chair to greet him, before realising that the dog's tone had not changed, as it usually did. Madge was still barking, but there was a sustained ferocity to it, warning her that danger lay ahead.

"Madge?" Gabi said, and took a step forward in the near darkness of the living room, before shrinking back again at the sound of a sickening blow, followed by the dog's whimper.

The barking stopped.

Gabi clapped a hand over her mouth to prevent a cry of distress escaping, and pressed herself behind the kitchen wall, where she had a view of the long, sliding glass door to the living room in the mirrored splashback.

That's when she saw the figure appear, and recognised it immediately.

"Gabrielle?"

Saffron stood inside the doorway, blocking the exit.

"Gabrielle? I know you're here. I just want to talk to you."

Gabi could see the limp figure of the dog lying on the floor beside the door, and tears leaked from the corners of her eyes.

Saffron Wallows was capable of anything.

"Come out, or stay hiding, but I have a proposition for you," Saffron was saying. "I know that's why you invited me down here, after all. I've been waiting to have an opportunity to talk to you, all evening. Why pretend otherwise?"

Gabi could hear Saffron moving about the living room, looking behind sofas and peering behind curtains.

"This is really very juvenile, Gabi, and I expected better of you, after so many years," she continued.

"Look, I'm sorry about what happened last December. I was angry with you, and I panicked, but I can see that was hasty, and I regret it. Why not let bygones be bygones, hmm? Let's look at this like grown-ups, shall we? I'm a commodity—a rare commodity—that's worth a lot to your former publishing house, to your friend, your former fiancé…to an awful lot of people, including you, I might add. You built a reputation from mine, so we're in this together."

I didn't know what you'd done, Gabi wanted to shout. *I'm nothing like you!*

"I'll make you a deal, Gabi. One that's well worth taking. I'll give you half of my advance—and you know *exactly* how much my advances are—if you agree to remain silent about my little…indiscretion. I admit, I was going through a dry patch, and suffering from writer's block, when this…nobody, sent me her manuscript. Imagine my surprise, when it turned out to be good!"

Saffron laughed, and Gabi sensed she was drawing near.

"Imagine my good fortune when that same nobody wound up dying of ovarian cancer, within the space of a few months! It felt like a gift, Gabi. I'm sure you can understand."

You're a fraud, Gabi thought. *A cheat, a liar, and guilty of attempted murder.*

"Some people are important, and some people aren't," Saffron said, and Gabi knew that, in another moment, she'd be upon her.

Her hand reached up to turn on the outside lights, and the sudden glare startled Saffron into turning and heading back outside, assuming that somebody had activated them from there.

Gabi took her chance and fled, stepping carefully over Madge's quiet body with the deepest of sorrow.

When Luke was finally able to make some progress on the roads, he put his foot down and drove with scant regard for the Highway Code in a bid to get back as quickly as he could, before the tide came in. After pulling into the car park and slamming out of the Land Rover, he ran down the pathway towards the beach, passing some of the guests who had enjoyed an evening at the bookshop and were blissfully unaware that anything might be amiss.

He made it to the bookshop in time to find Nell waving off the last of the guests, one of whom cast an interested eye over his person, while her partner scratched the edge of what he considered to be a very weak chin with fingers that held the worst of all things: a gold pinky ring.

Momentarily distracted by its gaudiness, he forced himself back to matters at hand.

"Where's Gabi?" he asked Nell, who had been on the cusp of laying into him on the subject of tardiness.

"Gabi? I assumed she'd sneaked off to be with you," she said, and her demeanour changed instantly to one of concern. "I haven't seen her for about half an hour."

"Is everything all right?" the woman asked. "Is Gabi ill, or something?"

They both ignored her.

"I'll try the house," Luke said, and turned on his heel to run, feet skidding against the pathway as he covered the ground at speed.

When Gabi stepped outside, she spotted Saffron blocking the main gate that led to the pathway running down to the cove, and she made a split-second decision, turning to run the other way.

Saffron heard the flash of movement across the lawn, and gave chase.

She would not lose, now. She would not surrender a single piece of all she had earned, and if there were to be sacrifices made along the way, she would do it for the greater good.

And she was the Greater Good.

Gabi burst through the exotic plants bordering Luke's garden, clawing her way through giant ferns and weeping vines, feet sinking into the rich soil as she made for the bottom of the cliff steps on the western edge of the cove. She knew they were visible from that side of the garden—she only needed to find them, unless she was able to reach somebody and raise the alarm, first.

But there was no time to think—she could hear Saffron's heavier tread trampling the undergrowth not far behind.

Leaves and branches tore at her skin and ripped through her hair, but she didn't stop, she kept on running, knowing only the fear of an animal that sensed when another, more dangerous and unpredictable beast was poised to strike.

Reaching the edge of the undergrowth, she came to a minor precipice, but it was too late to stop herself falling, this time to land in a painful heap at the foot of the cliff stairs. She dragged herself up, seconds before Saffron emerged from the trees and began to scramble upward, climbing the slippery pathway towards Gull's Point with single-minded focus.

"*Gabrielle!*"

She heard Luke's voice calling out into the night, and wished she could call back to him, but then she thought of what Saffron had done to the dog, and of how she'd been willing to let her die before the path of an oncoming train. She would have no qualms in hurting anyone she loved; she would consider them to be collateral damage, and nothing more.

And so, she drove herself onward, fingers gripping the limestone as her feet struggled to find purchase on the worn steps. Somewhere below, she heard Saffron breathing heavily, keeping pace with her all the way.

Gabi gritted her teeth and continued to climb, willing herself not to think about the height, or of her fate if she should lose her footing and fall. Her only thought was to reach the summit and then make for the car park, where she could raise the alarm.

She never made it that far.

For, as she reached a narrow plateau directly above the cave network where Madge had disappeared, she stepped into thin air, and her worst nightmare was realised.

She fell, down and down through a narrow shaft and into the depths of the cave below, her scream echoing out across the silent landscape.

Luke ran back down towards the beach, now frantic with worry.

"Any sign?" Nell demanded.

"None," he said, running a hand through his hair. "She isn't at the house, but the door was wide open and the dog had been attacked. I've made her comfortable, for now, but I think she's concussed."

Just then, they heard a scream penetrate the night air, and Luke took an involuntary step forward.

"That's her—that's Gabi!"

"Luke—wait! I'll get help!"

He didn't wait, but ran onto the beach, following the direction of her voice, only to find the tide was up to his shins already. If Gabrielle was trapped in the caves, there was no chance she would find her way out—she would be lost in there, as the tide drew in.

It would be like history repeating itself, and he wasn't prepared to let that happen.

He would not lose another woman he loved.

CHAPTER 37

Gabi landed in a heap on the wet sand, twisting her ankle badly and damaging her wrist, which bent backwards when she tried to brace her fall.

Soon after, she heard the shuffling sound of another person trying to edge their way down the shaft through which she'd fallen, and she hurried to get up and move away, before Saffron could find her. She ran blindly through the caves, her foot dragging behind her, until she felt the splash of water rising against her legs.

The tide.

Dragging air through her lungs, she felt her way along the walls of the caves, searching desperately for a scrap of light that might guide her towards the beach, and towards home.

"Gabrielle!"

She heard Saffron calling for her, and bore down, continuing onward, stumbling and tripping over the bits of wood and seaweed washed up from the ocean floor.

"Gabrielle!"

Another voice, this time.

Luke!

"Luke! I'm in here! In the caves!" she called out, and heard her voice echo around the walls.

Saffron heard it too, and Gabi heard her moving amongst the tunnels, searching for her.

Think, she told herself.

Think!

Where would be best to go? Where would be the most likely place Luke might find her?

But every tunnel looked just the same as the next.

They formed a human chain, leading all the way from the harbour. Every resident of the cove, and any remaining guests who could be prevailed upon to help—including Frenchie and Mark. Luke was at the head of them, wading out into the rising tide, calling out to the woman he had come to love, and who he was not willing to lose.

"Gabrielle!"

He waited, and thought he heard a faint answering cry, which was all he needed.

Letting go of the chain, he dived into the water and swam with powerful strokes towards the entrance of the caves.

The water had risen up to her waist.

Gabi tried to keep going, for warmth as much as anything else, following her instinct as to the direction of the cave entrance.

When Luke called out to her again, it seemed a little closer than before, and she struck out with renewed energy, splashing through the water to reach him.

"Luke!"

But it was not Luke who confronted her in the darkened tunnel.

"There you are," Saffron said. "I've been looking for you, everywhere."

She made a lunge for her in the darkness, and Gabi threw herself to one side, hearing the splash of Saffron's body connecting with the water somewhere to her right. Teeth chattering, she made a desperate bid to get away, arms and legs pushing past the pain, past the fear, towards the sound of his voice.

"Gabi! Where are you?"

"I'm here! I'm he—"

Saffron fell upon her from behind, and Gabi was submerged beneath the icy water.

Luke followed the sound of her voice and swam through the tunnels, following the map in his own mind, as water continued to rise all around him. There was not a scrap of light to help him, but he used his other senses, listening past the sound of the sea to the more subtle sound of thrashing limbs, as the two women rolled and kicked beneath the waterline.

He reached them, just in time.

Grabbing a fistful of hair, he pulled them apart, dragging Gabi upward but finding her limp, her body having taken on too much water. The other woman came for him again, lashing out in the darkness, and he threw her a glancing blow, his fist connecting with the edge of her face with enough force to send her sprawling back into the water.

He didn't stop to worry about it, but tucked an arm around Gabrielle and began kicking out towards the exit, relying on his memory as a guide. It was a gruelling journey, and his body shook with exhaustion against the force of the oncoming tide, but he would not stop.

He would never stop.

The Coastguard was waiting for him, when he emerged from the caves, and he would later have Nell to thank for having the presence of mind to call them in, before it was too late.

He collapsed onto the boat, and watched as they worked to check Gabrielle's airways, then heard her spluttering and coughing, expelling the water she'd inhaled during her struggle.

Only then did he crawl across to her, and cradle her in his arms.

"I'm never letting you go again," he wheezed.

Gabrielle didn't bother to argue, but curled her fingers around his and held on tightly until they reached the shore.

EPILOGUE

Saffron Wallows' body washed up several days later, horribly bloated and half-eaten by fish.

The PR team at Frenchman Saunders were disinclined to include that information in their official press release, nor the fact that her reputation and career had been an expensive lie. Gabrielle Adams set the record straight, providing her written testimony to every major broadsheet, both domestic and international, as well as the name of the woman who deserved to be remembered: Kelly Ann Smith.

By way of restitution, Wallows' publisher made an offer of money to Kelly's family, which was refused in lieu of a complete removal of all Wallows' work from general sale, and an agreement to publish a modest run of Smith's collected works, which went on to sell out within twenty-four hours.

Carnance Books & Gifts placed a significant first order of Smith's new release, and created a beautiful window display which they maintained for a full year.

Its manager, Gabrielle Adams-Malone, went on to write several books on the topic of mental health and wellbeing, which helped many people through dark times, and that was all the reward she'd ever needed.

Jackson Trelawney fell in love with a young man, and they live happily together in his mother's house, where she takes great pride in having gained another son.

Jude Barker continues to put on weight, thanks to his wife's superlative baking.

Mark and Frenchie were married and divorced, following his serial infidelity, and nobody was surprised.

AUTHOR'S NOTE

The storyline for *The Cove* was inspired by two events: the first was when I happened to read, one day, about a man who had taken it upon himself to push unsuspecting people onto the train tracks on the London Underground. The idea instantly evokes a feeling of horror—not only at the prospect that any one of us might have been unlucky enough to find ourselves the unwitting victim of such an attack, but at the thought of someone like him wandering the streets, melting into the crowd, waiting for the next moment to strike. I lived in London throughout my twenties, and, although not involved in publishing at that time, it was easy to imagine myself at that age, enjoying the city with very few cares in the world, and how different life would have been had it all come to a crashing halt, following such a life-changing event.

The second event was my happening to visit Kynance Cove, in Cornwall, with my husband and young son for the first time, around 2015 or 2016. We were charmed by its beauty, and lucky enough to visit at a time when we had the beach almost to ourselves. Its sand truly is golden, and the waters surrounding it are pure aquamarine. But it was the sudden storm which drew into the cove whilst we were there that sparked the idea for this novel. I remember sitting in the lovely café overlooking the water, huddled with my son on my lap, whilst we waited out the weather and I will always remember thinking that the thunder and lightning, the crashing waves, and the sense of real seclusion was awesome to behold. Of course, in my fictional story, I've changed its name to Carnance to remind the reader that all names, businesses and storylines included in *The Cove* are of my own making and are not based on any real persons, living or dead.

As for the publishing side to this story, I always think it's important to poke a little fun at oneself, from time to time, but I can assure you that I am nothing like some of the dastardly characters portrayed in this novel.

At least, I do hope not...

LJ ROSS
July 2021

New for 2026

Order now!

*There's nothing so deadly as the sea, and
the man who survives it . . .*

Clara Enys was finally living the dream. After years of grafting, she was the proud owner of Cornwall's newest restaurant, The Lizard, named for the peninsula upon which it sat, perched high on a clifftop overlooking the sea. When she wasn't whipping up culinary feasts, she volunteered at the nearby lifeboat station, serving as crew with a team who risked their lives regularly to save others. With no immediate plans to settle down, life was pretty much perfect.

When a distress signal comes through one stormy night from a luxury yacht, Clara is ready to answer the call. Too late to save the vessel, they search raging seas for survivors—but find only one . . .

A man with no name, no memory, and the capacity to turn her world upside down.

LOVE READING?

JOIN THE CLUB...

Join the LJ Ross Book Club to connect with a thriving community of fellow book lovers!

To receive a free monthly newsletter with exclusive author interviews and giveaways, sign up at www.ljrossauthor.com or follow the LJ Ross Book Club on social media:

@LJRossAuthor

@ljross_author

ABOUT THE AUTHOR

LJ ROSS is an international bestselling author known for her atmospheric mystery and thriller novels, including the DCI Ryan series which has sold over 12 million copies worldwide. Her debut novel *Holy Island* published in 2015 and reached number one in the Amazon UK and Australian digital charts. Louise has since released over thirty novels, most of which have been UK number one digital bestsellers. She is also the creator of the bestselling Dr Alexander Gregory series and the Summer Suspense series. Louise is a keen philanthropist and proud to support numerous non-profit programmes in addition to founding the Lindisfarne Prize for Crime Fiction, the Northern Photography Prize and the Northern Film Prize.

Born in Northumberland, England, she studied Law at King's College, University of London, then abroad in Florence and Paris, and worked as a lawyer before pursuing her dream to write. She lives with her family in Northumberland.

If you would like to get in touch with LJ Ross on social media, please scan the QR code below – she would love to hear from you!